DISCARDED
From Nashville Public Library

A Candle for St. Jude

Other Books by Rumer Godden

BLACK NARCISSUS

GYPSY, GYPSY

BREAKFAST WITH THE NIKOLIDES

TAKE THREE TENSES:
A Fugue in Time

THUS FAR AND NO FURTHER

THE RIVER

RUMER GODDEN

A Candle
for St. Jude

New York · 1948
THE VIKING PRESS

Part of this book appeared in the *Ladies' Home Journal*.

PRINTED IN U.S.A. BY THE COLONIAL PRESS INC.

A Candle for St. Jude

Chapter One

THIRTY years ago Madame Holbein had seen the wistaria and taken the house. "I didn't look at anything else," she said. "I didn't need to."

"You didn't look at the drains and *look* at the drains!" said Miss Ilse.

The wistaria grew over the coach-house that Madame had converted into the theatre. "It is a perfect setting. Perrfect! Those shutters! That scrolled-iron balcony above it! The wistaria!" It was, truthfully, like a stage wistaria; Madame almost felt indignant with it for not being in flower for her winter season in December. "There is not another like it in the whole of London," she said.

The theatre was the reason for the existence of the school. Madame had started it when she had retired from ballet those thirty years ago. It had been her brother Jan's idea, his dream that he did not live to see. "And he was spared a lot of trrouble, not?" said Madame. She had planned it as a self-contained unit, a theatre with its own company trained in its own school, self-contained, though small.

"Then I shall have it exactly as I want," Madame had said at the beginning. She was still discovering how wrong she had been. "It will be a nest-egg of ballet," she had said. "Something valuable."

"Valuable! How will you pay for it?" asked Miss Ilse.

Madame did not know. "Somehow," she said, and that was how it had been paid for ever since. The prudent Miss Ilse had often tried to make her lease it for other purposes. "You could have plays, small productions, Anna."

"Only ballet."

"Or films. Films pay."

"Only ballet."

"They could be French films, Anna."

"Only ballet."

"But, Anna, we shall be ruined."

"How can we be?" asked Madame. "I made the theatre small so that the expenses could be small."

"But they are not small. You take such risks."

"You don't understand," said Madame with dignity, and with more dignity she said, "It is economically necessary that I take risks." It might be said that it was. At all events, the theatre had survived. Its course had not been smooth, but then nothing with Madame was smooth. Like all theatrical enterprises it had had its storms and quarrels and mistakes and mishaps and opportunities taken and opportunities missed and accidents and triumphs and tears. A theatre is blooded in triumphs and tears. The thing that had held the slippery, rudimentary structure of this one together was the unshaken belief of Madame. It had not occurred to her to doubt. "You always were conceited, Anna," Miss Ilse said often. "Yes, I olways was," agreed Madame. She might tirade at the moment but she took little notice of those triumphs or of tears. She made mistakes—"Ah! hundreds of them!" said Madame, but immediately added, "And most people would have made hundreds more!"—but on the whole, through the years, she had been miraculously right. " 'Miraculously' is correct," said Madame gravely. "Olways at the eleventh minute something comes along to save me, not?" "I don't know how you do it!" people exclaimed to Madame. Often she did not know either.

Her theatre was a miniature one, her company young, from her own school. "But they take me seriously," said Madame. "It is not a pupils' show." Twice every year, in May, "when the wistaria is out, full," said Madame, and before Christmas, a little part of London came to Hampstead and she gathered her small influential public. She never took her company to other theatres, she never took it on tour. "No. It was designed for this small stage," she said. "It shall stay where it is, at home."

She complained that her pupils used her, that they left just as she had matured them: "Oll the years of worrk and care, one season and then, tchk-tchk!" said Madame. " 'Good-bye, Madame, thank you verry much,' and off they go."

"That is your reward," said Mr. Felix.

Madame looked at him. Was he speaking bitterly or stating a fact? It was bitter and it was a fact; that was her reward. She still complained.

"But, Madame, wouldn't you have felt cramped and cheated if you had had to dance always on such a tiny stage?" That was Lion.

"I should have been glad to have the chance," said Madame haughtily.

"To begin with, yes . . ."

"Besides, my dearr Lion, you can't compare me. That is rridiculous! I needed a big company, a big audience, a big stage. I could fill it."

"Doesn't every dancer feel that?"

"But often it is not trrue."

"Sometimes it is," said Lion.

Of course they used her. Everyone who came near her used her. "Everyone wants something," she would sometimes say when she had grown exhausted, and nowadays she was frail. "Keep them away, Ilse. Shut the door. Let me not see anyone today. They are oll selfish, inconsiderate. Oll of them want—want—want! None of them have anything to give." Miss Ilse was happy when Madame needed her but, of course, none of it was quite true. Madame gave, but she was an arch-taker; she took from them all, from Miss Ilse, Mr. Felix, from Lion; particularly and skilfully from every male she knew, from Leonid Gustave, the giant of the ballet world, down to her smallest pupil, Archie, whom she called Khokhlik[1] because of his tuft of hair.

[1] *Russian for a crest or tuft. Also used as an endearment.*

She took from the whole of life. How else was she to give?

Miss Ilse Holbein was not a participant in the Holbein Theatre and Ballet School; she was a part.

To make confusion worse, Miss Ilse was Madame Holbein, while Madame was Miss; Miss Ilse had married Jan Holbein, Madame's elder brother; Anna, Madame, had not married at all. "I did not need to," said Madame.

"No," agreed Miss Ilse, and said no more.

"One must be adult in these things," Madame said. "Besides," she said with a twinkle in her otherwise grave eyes, "I have olways said you can have your cake and eat it."

On a table in Miss Ilse's office in the school was a pair of Jan Holbein's shoes under a glass dome, and his death mask. The small pupils in the school dared not be left alone with that still marble face, and they wondered how Miss Ilse could turn her back on it and sit calmly at her desk writing Madame's notes and adding up the household accounts. The truth was that Miss Ilse felt he was scarcely to do with her; if she had been married to Jan, both of them had been married to Madame's career; Jan had been Anna Holbein's teacher and adviser till the day of his death, though he was a fine dancer and choreographer in his own right. "He never was mine. He was all for Anna," said Miss Ilse. She said it without rancour; she belonged to Madame too. Her heart and body and mind were given to Madame; her soul, firmly, to God through the medium of the Catholic Church, in particular the Church and Convent of the Presentation, opposite the school; it did not occur to her that she had nothing left for herself, but moments of depression came on Miss Ilse when everything she had been taught to believe seemed to her wrong. She had tried to be the things she felt she should be: gentle, considerate, unselfish, patient, and as truthful as she could, and yet she had little of life while Madame, who was wilful, inconsiderate, passionate, and not always strictly truthful, had life in abundance.

"I like life whole, in the rround," said Madame. "I . . . welcome it. Oll! I don't want to, how do you say, *dodge* any of it. I think that is important."

"Then why are you always grumbling?" asked Miss Ilse.

"My grumbling is part of the whole," said Madame haughtily. "Besides, I don't agree. I don't grumble."

"But you do, Anna. You grumble at everything: at the east wind, at the soup, at your time-table, at your exercises, at the children."

"Then I have to. To balance what I love. I love so many things."

"What things?" asked Miss Ilse suspiciously.

"Universal things," said Madame dreamily. "You would not understand, but I shall explain to you. Universal things that are for everybody and things that are for me, personally," said Madame with dignity. "I olways feel, for instance, that red and white roses together are for me. Don't ask me why. They are for me. Yes, red and white roses, and then, the Gulf Stream."

"The Gulf Stream, Anna?"

"Yes. We in England ought to love the Gulf Stream. It

keeps us from being frozen . . . quite. And I love spires
and may trees, and views, some views; and houses, some
houses; I love mahogany and the smell of spices; *peculiarly*
I love the smell of spices, and food, the taste of that salmon
at lunch, out of season, not? And poems. I love that poem
about the deer by . . . by? . . . We had wine at lunch
and that is why I think of him (and tomorrow we shall
lunch on poached eggs and coffee, not? That is life) . . .
Drrinkwater, that is his name. I love his poem. I love so
much, everything; this minute. And today . . ." She shut
her eyes. "Today, say, anemones in flower."

"But anemones are not in flower. They are over long
ago."

"That makes not the slightest difference," said Madame.

"Sometimes, Anna, you behave like a child. Or a young
girl."

"I am a young girl," said Madame, with her eyes still
shut. "I am what I was for ever. So are you, Ilse, but you
have forgotten. I don't forrget. I am what I am, each moment, for ever." . . . Time passes, that is what they say,
thought Madame, but that is what it cannot do . . .

Above the fireplace in the first-class room downstairs was
a photograph in a large oval frame, one among the hundreds of photographs all through the house. This was of
a girl with dark ringlets in a small-waisted, full-skirted,
scallop-flounced white dress painted with cherries: Madame, the dancer Anna Holbein, as Columbine in *Carnaval*.

"But they do *Carnaval now!*" one of the smallest pupils exclaimed.

"Yes . . . and I saw a company here in London use a blue painted back-drrop instead of the Bakst frieze and curtains," snapped Madame.

"But . . . if they couldn't get them, Anna? Things are difficult since the war," said Miss Ilse.

"Then don't do it at oll. Better to let it be lost than turned to a trravesty. Where is the poetry? Where is the rrichness? I ask you."

"Anna, I beg you. Don't get excited."

"I am not in the *least* excited. I am perrfectly calm."

Even Madame's illusions were personal. For instance, she believed that she was serene. "A dancer should give serenity," she told each pupil. "She must set her audience at rrest, dear child. She must be calm."

"Then why isn't she?" the pupil might have said.

Madame loved and cherished her little theatre.

It was at the side of the house, opening on the Avenue; it ran back into the garden and here she had built the stage. Its frontage was only the width of old stables, and its glassed entrance had been made where the harness-room door had been, with the scrolled-iron balcony above it on which the wistaria had spread along the front and on to the wall.

The theatre had been blasted in the war and all its glass broken. "But there never was much glass," said Madame obstinately.

"Yes. It always was a stuffy little hole," agreed Lion.

"Stuffy—little—hole!"

But it had had to close. Now Lion had arranged for the glass to be mended and the cracks in the walls to be repaired. He made Madame apply for a permit, "and for redecorating as well," said Lion.

"Not redecorating," contradicted Madame. "It is to stay exactly as it is. Repainting, that is oll."

"You will need a permit for that."

"A permit! To paint my own theatre!" Finally he, and Glancy, who for years had been stage carpenter and electrician, and some of the male students, painted it themselves.

A whisper began to run through the school. The theatre was to be lent to the Spanish Dancers, to the Harlem Ballets Nègres, to the Balmont Company. "To anyone but ourselves," the pupils said disconsolately.

"How could we open? We haven't a company?" said Alma.

"We are the beginnings of a company ourselves." That was the ambitious restless Hilda.

"You are mad about that theatre," said Alma.

"Yes I am," said Hilda broodingly. She looked across the garden to the private door from the school to the theatre that was still locked. "We have Liuba Rayevskaya. We have John," she argued. "They are quite ready—and Lion would get the Metropolitan to release him to dance with us for a short season."

"It would have to be Lion *and* Caroline," Alma reminded her, and Hilda was silent.

"We are ready," she whispered rebelliously. She was more than ready. She was overdue.

Then Madame made an announcement. She was reopening the theatre for a five weeks' season, "My usual weeks in May," and the opening night was to coincide with the anniversary of her debut, fifty years ago. "It will be my jubilee," Madame explained. "Only I do *not* like that worrd. And you will give me a very special performance, not?" As special as you can, she thought, you are oll young untried dancers, though Lion and Caroline will be here. "Fifty years ago I made my debut," said Madame, "though I had danced many times before that at the Maryinsky but, of course, unnamed, and we were olways taken strraight home after we had done our parrt. Once I was named," said Madame, and she smiled. "But I was so small you would hardly notice me. That was before even I went to Russia, when I was with Jan, my brother, in Buenos Aires, and I danced the Humming-Bird in a ballet he had arranged there and that I shall revive for you this season, perhaps even on the opening night. Yes, I think on the opening night," said Madame. "It will be my diamond jubilee, if you must say jubilee, of that. I was seven," said Madame, and she added, with a twinkle, "Now at last you know how old I am."

Rehearsals had begun. "But we shan't be in it," said the youngest ones in the Beginners' Class. They had not been told any of this. It did not concern them, but they knew. News did not filter down to the Beginners' Class; they had a telegraph system of their own which knew everything

long before their elders; its wires kept buzzing and humming and tapping and vibrating; the most startling messages
were delivered continually and, if there had been any en-
velopes, they would have been the brightest possible orange.
Now it was flashed through the class that one of them was
to be chosen for that part of Madame's, the Humming-Bird
in Jan Holbein's ballet *Cat Among the Pigeons*. "It will be
Archie," said the Intelligence Department in the Beginners'
Class. It was Archie.

Though the theatre was miniature, it was real. The old
coach-house was the auditorium. Lion had repainted its
walls; they were cream with small gilt sconces that Madame
had had regretfully to electrify. "But it's better," said Miss
Ilse. "Those candles were far too hot; and they had to be
snuffed and relighted."

"That was part of the fascination."

"And their smell was horrid."

"Their smell was lovely and exciting," said Madame. "I
infinitely regrret those candles."

At first she had been afraid that the seating must be
chairs. "It will look like a school hall or a chapel," she had
said. But Miss Ilse, staying away at the seaside, as she liked
to do and Madame did not, had heard of a pier theatre
closing down and had sent an urgent message to Madame,
who had come down from London and bought thirty rows
of seats, red plush with red arms. Madame adored those
seats.

Cream walls, gilt sconces, red plush seats; she added a

small orchestra pit with a brass rail and curtains of Indian
cotton that hung in heavy pleats and were garishly pat-
terned in blue and crimson on a cream ground. She had her
own Bechstein from the drawing-room moved in. "But the
upright would have done," wailed Miss Ilse. The stage curtains were blue velvet, worn and faded now, their cords and
fringes red. The stage itself was fitted with side curtains and
a back-drop of plain greenish grey, "Because often we must
do without sets," Madame had said, but, so far, she had
never done without sets. The stage, built out into the garden, was properly fitted, of suitable height, and had a sloped
floor of soft pine. "As good to dance on as any anywhere,"
declared Madame. She knew. She had had to dance on
every kind of floor. There was a full range of lights from the
first old-fashioned battens and footlights to the recently
imported spots and floods. Lion had found a young man,
Edwin, and Madame had coaxed him into doing the lights;
now he did little else. Besides Edwin there was Glancy, the
stage carpenter, electrician, and house gardener, though
Madame gave him little time for gardening, and Emile,
Zanny's husband, who helped in the house and acted as
porter and commissionaire when the theatre was open.
Then, too, there was a girl for the box-office, and Miss
Parkes the secretary's married sister who came as a pro-
gramme-seller and usherette; there was an extra hand to
help Glancy on the stage itself, and behind the scenes there
were Zanny and Miss Porteus, the timid little red-nosed
dressmaker who made many of the dresses and, between

times, was expert in making tutus for the girls in the school.

The stables themselves had been converted into dressing-rooms, a loose-box for the men, another for the girls, while the stalls made cubicles for two principals. The flat and loft above had been turned into a wardrobe-room, with dresses hung along rods behind green curtains and properties in dress baskets down the centre. A big sewing table was pushed against the window and beside it stood a treadle sewing-machine and ironing-boards; the girls helped Zanny and Miss Porteus iron and mend the dresses. The floor was always littered with snippets and ends of tarlatan and gauze. Here Miss Porteus spent most of her day. Here she and Zanny had often worked far into the night before the seasons. "That has not happened for five years now," said Zanny. "No," said Miss Porteus with her perpetual little sniff. "I don't know how I should do it now, I am sure. My arthritis wasn't bad then. When it gets into my hands I shan't be able to sew." Miss Porteus wore a little hard black velvet pincushion pinned to the left breast of her dress in the shape of a heart. To her niece, Lollie, it seemed that it was Miss Porteus' heart, withered and worn, stuck with sharp pins. Madame would have added, "Filled with sawdust instead of good red blood," but that was too old a thought for Lollie, who worried about her aunt. Lollie had come to live with Miss Porteus so that she could work with Madame; Madame had seen her for the sake of Miss Porteus; she kept her for her own. "I wonder what she will become," said Madame. "She may end up with a rabbit face like Miss Porteus or she may have beauty."

The theatre box-office was in what had been the harness-room, that, painted and given a deep red carpet and gilt chairs, made a foyer.

As well as the drawing-room piano, Madame had taken the drawing-room chandelier; it hung in the foyer and made Miss Ilse feel sad every time she saw it. As soon as they found anything for a home, Madame took it away. "How can we ever hope to have a home?" said Miss Ilse.

The chandelier, to Madame, gave the last right finish. "Yes, I was rright about it," she said. "Ab-so-lute-ly right."

In May, the smell of the wistaria came in over the smell of wax and gauze and canvas and dust and grease-paint on to the stage itself; the mauve pendulums hung over the balcony and along the wall. "And that wistaria can change its character," said Madame. "It can be Japanese, tantalizing, hanging like lanterns; it can be the Rhine and love-songs and *Carnaval*; it can be English of cool green summers and meadows; it can grow on old brick walls, by the river, or on London sooted stone. I was ab-so-lute-ly rright about the wistaria," said Madame.

With the coach-house, of course, went the house. The house was always secondary to the theatre. "But . . . we want a home," said Miss Ilse.

"Anyone can have a home," said Madame.

"Anyone but I," Miss Ilse might have said.

Miss Ilse loved orderliness and light and white curtains

and the more delicate flowers. Sometimes she could not bear the very richness of the big dark house. Other people did not have houses like this, with its size and the dirtiness that came from its size, "And never enough servants," said Miss Ilse, "and the windows are so big they are *impossible* to keep clean." She was distressed by the crowd in it, the heterogeneous tongues and customs, the continual noise and hurry, and Madame's swift changes of mind, and the children leaving their shoes on the stairs and Zanny, Madame's old dresser, now her maid and despot wardrobe-mistress in the little theatre, who never did as she was asked or told. No, the house had never succeeded in establishing itself as a house; it was wiped out, first by the theatre, then by its characters.

It stood on its high North London ridge looking down on other roofs and streets, in tiers and crescents below it. It stood in trees. There was a recreation ground on one side that in spring had lilac and laburnum and pink may and chestnut trees, and on its other was the Avenue, with stucco houses that had flights of steps leading up to their front doors and laurels and shrubs in their front gardens. The house itself was grey and mammoth, with a double line of full-length windows that had wooden shutters from which all the paint had peeled and that had now the look of decay seen on the wood of some old river houses.

When Madame bought it, its garden had been neglected. Miss Ilse had cherished all kinds of plans for the garden but it was neglected still. It had a rough circular lawn in the middle of which stood a leaden basin with a fountain; it was useful for posing photographs but the fountain was broken. A path ran round the lawn, its asphalt was cracked and green with moss. By the house there were holly bushes; above them creepers hung from the balcony and the steps that led from the ground floor to the garden; they made the dark basement dressing-rooms under them darker still. Along the walls was a tangle of shrubs and plants. Glancy was supposed to take care of them, but Glancy had no time. If he kept the front in reasonable order, that was as much as he could do and, Miss Ilse had to admit, Madame was always calling him away for something else. The students ate their sandwiches in the garden in summer and were allowed to sit on the grass and sun-bathe if there were any sun and if Madame were out. Madame liked to look down from her windows and see its green; it was green, even if it had no flowers, and she preferred to see it empty. She liked to open the windows in spring to let in the smell of lilac even though it was always blended with the smell of cinders and cats.

Along the end and front walls there were plane trees and poplar trees that shed their different sizes of leaves in the garden and on the pavements; the plane-tree leaves turned brown or mottled brown and green, the poplars a bright clear yellow. "They are like bass and treble notes," said Hilda.

Music from the dancing school went over the wall into the road and the sounds of the road broke into the music:

cars passed, buses, horses, footsteps on the pavement, voices, and the voices of sparrows, but the children's voices on the stairs often sounded like sparrows.

Madame and Miss Ilse were so conditioned to living with music that neither of them heard it but, if Madame had listened, each piece or repeat or motive or end or tag had its association.

"You don't hear music as music any more," Mr. Felix accused her.

"I do!"

"No, it isn't possible for you . . . You never did," said Mr. Felix. "You understand nothing about music at all."

"What nonsense!" cried the indignant Madame. "It was brred in me."

"You should have been bred in it," said Mr. Felix. "No. You distort it, and colour it until it isn't music. You would have driven me mad," said Mr. Felix, "if I had been any-one else . . . and if you had been anyone else," he added under his breath.

"I know you," said Mr. Felix sternly to Madame. "You like the conventional, the pretty, the traditional, only you exaggerate it and say 'trraditional.' "

"You are very rrude," said Madame.

"The evening breeze," said Mr. Felix, "the pastorale; the ball, the petite; the white wreath, the Glinka waltz; and you can *not* free it from association."

She had to admit it. To associate is to be with another, with someone, something else. "Yes, to me music is the dance; that is trrue," said Madame. Sometimes it was a dance, simply; sometimes, someone in a dance; sometimes, very often, that other was herself. That is my *Impromptu,* said Madame, listening. *The Folly Impromptu.* I remember the little pink gloves I wore, apple-blossom pink. That is Bianca's *Tarantella,* with those red petticoats. That *Tarantella* belonged to Bianca. I could never give it to anyone else, but, perhaps, one day, someday, I shall find someone for it. That is the dance of the Wilis from *Giselle,* second act, and that is my *pas de deux* with Jan; I remember it in Madrid with Serge too. I taught it to Lydia and Paul; that hurt me, but I couldn't bear it to be lost. They are dancing it still in New York. I might give it to Francis and Liuba. It would suit Liuba, not? Caroline is not . . . saucy enough, said Madame. That is *Clair de Lune,* but I call it a cascade. Yes. I have olways the idea of a water-fall from that. Why a waterfall from moonlight? I don't know, but it comes from a thread of sound, like a question, like a source. Or do I mean a stream? asked Madame but no, her mind was obstinate, she meant a source that grew to a cascade. That is the laurel-wreath dance I taught to the children, thought Madame, listening. That is *Epiphany Hymn.* That ballet was a failure. It was Lion's first and only attempt at choreography. "It failed," said Madame. "And it cost you five hundred pounds," said Miss Ilse.

"Lion doesn't understand music. He shouldn't write ballets," said Mr. Felix. "He can dance them . . . if they are explained to him," he said not very kindly.

"Nonsense. Lion is quite musical."

"Quite musical people shouldn't experiment with music," said Mr. Felix acidly, and he added, "There is only one of you here who has that understanding."

"Caroline has exceptional feeling."

"None of Caroline's feelings are exceptional. I was talking of Hilda."

"Hilda! She plays, yes, but she doesn't play so very well."

"She knows more than she plays, then. I have never heard her play. She doesn't know yet what she knows." He paused and then said, "She is old. I call her the Egyptian."

"That isn't in the least like Hilda. Egyptian is another name for gypsy."

"Not that kind of an Egyptian. It is odd, sometimes, that you should be so stupid," said Mr. Felix most politely.

The house vibrated from the passing of the buses in the road and vibrated from the thud-leap-thud of the classes in its rooms. The buses were reflected in its mirrors, with the sky and leaves and the dancers in the rooms. The buses passed horizontally across while the leaves fell longitudinally, in and out of the mirrors' compass, in and out. Nothing had an end in those mirrors. Their frames were tarnished now, some of them were fly-blown, but they had kept their clarity. They reflected the rooms over and over again, as they reflected the dancers, as they had reflected other dancers, and others before them, one to another, and one to another again, and again: feet and legs and hands and arms and hips and waists and shoulders and heads; each, in its turn, was sharp, defined, and clear in the mirrors. "But you shouldn't look in the mirrors too much," said Madame. "You must feel. Feel to the tips of your fingers."

She said this to the small ones of the low division of the Beginners' Class, struggling with their five positions with Rebecca Clarke, her assistant.

"Your positions are like do, re, mi, fa that you sing in a scale; all your dancing will be based on them. You must learn them," said Rebecca.

"You must *feel* them," corrected Madame. "Zoë! why are you waving your hands like that? It is very prretty but it is not dancing. What are you thinking? You are thinking of something else, not of your *fouetté* at all."

She said it to her Advanced pupils, most of them taller than herself. "What you are doing now is verry likely more difficult than anything you will be called to do on the stage," she told them. "But it is far more difficult to feel it on the stage, I warn you. You not only have to prresent your dance, you have to give yourself to it as well. You must have temperrament." Madame's eyes would look along their ranks as if searching for that temperament among them. "Your audience should remember you when they have forrgotten how you danced." It was Hilda who heard the sadness in Madame's voice as she said that.

A dancer shouldn't grow old, thought Hilda. It is better if they die young; but, if Madame had died, thought Hilda, there would have been no Ballet Holbein and no theatre. Both were extremely necessary to Hilda at this time.

The front door of the dancing school was not the front door of the house. It was found by a process of elimination or divination. It was not the side door, nor the door to the left of the side door that led into the cellars; many mothers had found themselves first in the cellars; "And I wish some of them could have stayed there," said Madame. It was a door round at the back that had once been the garden door of the house. Here was a bell-pull that was broken. "Really, we must get the bell mended," said Miss Ilse, but, every time, Madame put it off. Miss Ilse suspected she preferred the bell broken. "Well, it is less disturbing," said Madame.

New pupils, new mothers, and visitors stood on the door-step timidly expectant, wondering why nobody heard them and if they dared walk in.

They could have walked in, almost at any time, because, in winter, as in summer, the door was nearly always open. "What a drraught! Go and shut the outside door!" was one of Madame's most frequent commands, but, however often it was shut, it was sure, almost immediately, to be left open again.

It opened into the dressing-rooms, three grimy crowded dark basement rooms with windows on the garden that were overhung by the creepers from the balcony above. One dressing-room was for the boys and young men, one for girls, and one for little girls. Men and boys were supposed to use the flight of steps that led up into the hall above, but they liked to slip through the girls' room to the back staircase where the oilcloth was worn away to strands and only the brass treads were left. Here they all sat, and read, or learnt their notes or ate buns and sweets and chattered. They were not supposed to talk, but they talked, and every evening Miss Ilse picked up toffee papers and newspapers and tufts of the wool the girls used in their blocked shoes and often two or three pairs of shoes as well. "Very dangerous!" Miss Ilse would say, "with all the ribbons left hanging," and she would pin them on the notice-board she had put up in the hall, though Madame usually left her notices on the piano or in her pocket.

Each room had a big table in the centre and pegs and pigeon-holes along the walls with benches under them; on the tables, in the pigeon-holes, on the pegs, was always a conglomeration of objects: hats and coats and gloves and bags and tunics and scarves and socks and tights; sandwiches in paper bags, buns, bottles of milk and lemonade; parts of costumes; tambourines, newspapers, music, cheap *attaché* cases, powder puffs; and shoes, always shoes, pink, white, black, green, blocked, unblocked; red character shoes, black shoes with red heels; and always shoe ribbons, entangled on the tables, under the tables, and hanging from the pigeon-holes. The air smelled of soot and powder and rosin, of garlic from the sausage the Italian boys, Lippi and Giacomo, brought in for lunch; of acid-drops and gas. The whole big old-fashioned house smelled of gas.

There were two classrooms on the ground floor, huge rooms that had been the dining- and drawing-rooms. They ran the width of the house, from front to back, with windows looking over the front wall through the plane trees to the buses, and to the garden over the balcony at the back.

The rooms were old now. Three decades of dancers had taken their steps on the floors that now had an imperishable dust compounded of rosin and of old wood that was never polished. The ceilings had kept their gilt but their white paint had yellowed and cracked, and the old embossed paper on the walls had relapsed into uniform brownness. The light in the rooms, made greenish and soft by the trees outside, was darkened still more by the walls and struck the glass in the photograph frames as gently as it struck the mirrors.

No house ever had as many photographs. They were five or six deep in each room along the walls, over the mantel-pieces, some even high up over the doors . . . But those must be the ones Madame thought nothing of, thought Hilda. . . . They were in the hall, in the office, up the stairs. Some, very old and yellow, were in the dressing-rooms. Archie had drawn beards and moustaches on some of the women and given breasts to some of the men. When he came to a Columbine in the corner he saw that some-one, long ago, had been before him and given her whiskers round her mouth in Prussian blue.

The *barres* were blackened and smoothed by those three decades of hands, the stuffing had split the red rep in the seats under the windows, the pianos had become kettle-drums, and still the work went on. "No! We are too shabby.

It is disgraceful," said Madame. "We must have the rrooms redone." And then, when Miss Ilse had made the arrangements, she said in surprise, "But how can I, *now*, while we are so busy?"

Madame's colours were red and gold and, like Miss Ilse, white, but the difference was the difference between muslin and snow.

On the first floor were Madame's own rooms. Miss Ilse shared Madame's, which meant she herself had none. Here were Madame's colours in the white and gilt papers, red carpets, and gilt frames of mirrors. "Don't you have enough of mirrors downstairs?" asked Miss Ilse. "I am used to mirrors," said Madame.

There was gilt on handles and doorplates and more red in the flowers Madame liked to buy herself. "The money you spend on those flowers, we could have bought a little house for ourselves with it!" "I am used to flowers," said Madame, "and I don't like little houses." The white was in the flowers too, and in the long net curtains; the furniture was of Madame's favorite wood, mahogany.

Miss Ilse polished it herself with a cloth wrung out in boiling water and vinegar. "My mother taught me that, *not* to use furniture polish," said Miss Ilse. One day she read that that was how good wood was treated in old Japan and China. It made her curiously happy. Now, when she looked at the wistaria, which anyhow made her think always of Japan, she felt she had a defiant little secret of her own.

Madame's rooms had a collection of what the students

called "relics." There was a great frame of newspaper cuttings from all over the world, another of programmes. There were Madame's first blocked shoes, kept like Jan's, and looking like two soiled pink sugar mice under their glass dome. There was a cast, in bronze, of her foot; in a cabinet, the cloak and swansdown muff she had worn in *Snowflakes;* a lace frill off a bouquet, and the filigree holder that had held it; a chocolate box that the Tsar had given her as a child at the Imperial School, "Oll the children had one, but I kept mine"; a fan from the Empress of Austria; an opal from the people of Sydney; and, among all these, the white kid collar of her dead cat, Pomponette.

Each was a memento of something that had happened, tender, triumphant, sorrowful, or gay, but always exciting, in her life. She could not bear to part with one of them. The students called them her "relics": *that which is left after loss or decay of the rest*—but, more than they knew, they were relics in another sense: *personal memorials to be held in reverence and an incentive to faith.* If they had had them they would have treasured them equally. Only they would not have had so many, said Madame.

Chapter Two

THE sound of the evening Angelus fell with a gentle peremptoriness into the office where Miss Ilse sat answering Madame's personal notes. Miss Parkes, the secretary, answered the rest, but so many of Madame's notes were personal. "To be imperrsonal is to be dull," said Madame, but to be very personal can be wearisome. Miss Ilse sighed.

"Dear General Cook Yarborough," she wrote, *"Madame Holbein asks me to tell you she has not the least intention . . ."*

"Ding. Ding-dong," went the bell. Miss Ilse underlined *least,* it made it sound more like Madame, and laid down her pen and stood up.

"Hail Mary, full of grace . . ." She shut her eyes, her lips moved.

"Blessed art Thou . . ." The words and thought were like dew to someone parched with the heat of the day, and the day had been at white-heat with Madame. *"And blessed is the fruit . . ."*

The telephone rang.

"Of Thy womb, Jesus." Miss Ilse continued steadily.

"Ding. Ding-dong." *"Hail Mary . . ."*

The telephone rang again.

"Ilse, can't you not answer that telephone?"

"The Lord is with Thee." Miss Ilse put out her hand and laid the receiver down beside the telephone on the desk. *"Blessed art Thou . . ."*

Madame came in angrily but stopped when she saw Miss Ilse standing with her eyes shut and her lips moving. Though so gentle, Miss Ilse was like a stone in her religion. She would admit no other.

"But oll are good," argued Madame. "The Buddhists . . ." She saw a Buddhist as a little man, not unlike Mr. Felix, her old pianist, with a Buddha face, smooth and ageless; a little man sitting on a remote mountain, above cloud, watching the world turning below, as complete and detached from him as the circle of his prayer-wheel. "How restful!" said Madame. "But naturally. It is olways easier to do anything without emotion . . . if you can, but then, emotion is so interresting," said Madame. She loved the fire and singleness of the Mohammedans. "Islam, one God, the mosque that is empty of everything but prayer, the whole world of faith in a prayer-mat; the sword; the discipline of the month of fast. It is a man's faith," said Madame. "And Hinduism is rrich and intangible and strange, not easily to be understood, and that is intriguing; and in Confucius there is such sense. I can understand fire-worship," said Madame, who was always shivering. "And sun-worship; and the worship of ancestors. That is trradition," said Madame. "A dancer reverences tradition, *peculiarly*," said Madame. "And my own Russian Orthodox Church, so old and filled with beauty; but to hear Ilse," said Madame, "you would think that there is only one in the whole wide world, her own."

"Only one," said Miss Ilse.

"You are narrow. Bigoted."

"I can't help it. That is what I believe."

"I don't understand you."

It had not occurred to Madame that dancing was her religion and she was remarkably intolerant about it. "Ilse, and her Saints and her prayers," said Madame, but she who ruled Miss Ilse had not been able to stop her slipping over the way to see the nuns or light a candle or say a prayer at one time or another, for one thing or another, in all the ups and downs of their life; to St. Anthony, on all the occasions that Madame lost her purse, or the key of the safe; to St. Michael when she was ill; to the Little Flower. The Saints, their merits and attributes, were clear and consistent, while the people who thronged the house and school and theatre, these balletomanes and dancers and artists and actors and poets, from the producers to the pupils, were all so muddled and unhappy, so feverish and contradictory, that Miss Ilse could never arrive at understanding one of them; and Madame . . . "But then," said Miss Ilse, "she is always the same, or never the same for ten minutes together!" Miss Ilse said prayers for a great many people, but the most of her candles and prayers were for Madame.

Once, long ago, for instance, in Copenhagen . . . "Yes, it was in Copenhagen," said Miss Ilse, who often told this to the children, "the winter of nineteen-eleven, just after Christmas. I remember how beautiful the snow was, and the Square, and the green spires of the churches, and the sleighs coming in from the country to market, and the early copper sunsets. There was a sleighing party and I asked Anna not to go. I had a foreboding . . .

"Anna. You shouldn't go. I feel it in my bones."

"Don't be a fool, Ilse."

"Don't go, Anna. Don't go. I beg of you. Not on a Gala night."

"I am going with . . ." Miss Ilse could not remember his name, but she saw him clearly still: young brown eyes and brown moustaches and black frogging on his great-coat.

"Anna. He drives so fast."

"They oll drive fast."

"Suppose there is an accident."

"Tchk-tchk! Why should there be an accident?"

"It is a command performance, Anna. Suppose you couldn't dance. Anna . . . if the sleigh overturns!"

"Why should it overturn?" But it did, as Miss Ilse had mysteriously known it would, and Madame's foot was caught and bruised. She stormed and wept and pleaded, but it was hopeless. The placards outside the theatre announcing the Gala performance in the presence of the King and Queen had her name, ANNA HOLBEIN, in large letters, but Madame could not stand on her foot. How could she dance?

Zanny was with them. "Zanny was *always* with us," said Miss Ilse in annoyance; and, of course, Zanny knew best and pushed Miss Ilse aside and ran out to a cabmen's eating-house near by and came back with an apron of hot potatoes. "Hot potatoes for bruises," said Zanny.

"I never heard of such a thing," said Miss Ilse, but Zanny pushed her aside again and opened potato after potato and applied them, like poultices, to the foot. Miss Ilse pressed her lips together . . . she pressed her lips together now . . . and took down her cloak from behind the door where Zanny had hung it out of the way. She remembered it, a dark-blue cloak with a narrow sealskin collar cut from an old muff of Madame's.

"Where are you going, Ilse?" Miss Ilse had preferred not to say in front of Zanny and had gone silently out into the twilit snow. She remembered how foreign the streets had seemed in that half light, how dim and cold, with a hustle that confused her more in the confusion of her worry about Madame, but she had found what she had been looking for, a church, and in it the Saint she was looking for. "St. Jude," said Miss Ilse, and she smiled, remembering. "Yes. I lighted my candle to him there."

"St. Jude. Why St. Jude?" asked Madame scornfully,

trying her shoe, and biting her lips with the pain. "It's no good, Ilse. I can't dance."

"St. Jude is the saint of lost causes, Anna. Try again."

"St. Jude!" said Madame more scornfully, but presently, after more poulticing, she was able to stand in her shoe, presently to stand on her *pointes,* to turn, then to warm up a little and, finally, though in pain, to dance. The lace up-stairs in the cabinet, the filigree holder, was from a bouquet she had that night. "Was it from the Queen?" asked Miss Ilse. "Or did the Queen send the bracelet? I remember something from the Queen, or was it that young man with the moustaches? Did he send the bracelet or the bouquet?" She did not know, but she knew Madame had danced that night.

"It was the potatoes," said Zanny.

"It was St. Jude," said Miss Ilse.

Now in the office Madame looked at Miss Ilse with irrita-tion and disdain, but she answered the telephone.

"Was it anything important?" asked Miss Ilse when the last sound of the Convent bell had died away and she had stood for a moment as if she were reluctant to let it go. She sighed as she opened her eyes. "The telephone hasn't been quiet all day."

"What do you expect, the day before the opening?" Mad-ame said crossly. "Ilse, you are one of the people who would pray while Jericho was falling."

"It was Edmund White," she said. "You know, *the* Ed-mund White." Miss Ilse shook her head. "Don't be a fool,

Ilse. The prroducer. Broadwood Studios. He says he will give Lollie an audition, here, tomorrow at four. I said he should see her in the theatre."

"In the *theatre!* The *afternoon* of the *opening!* Well, *really*, Anna!"

"It should be empty then."

"They will be doing the flowers."

"They can stop doing the flowers for a little while. I know Edmund. It will only take a few minutes."

"And how do you know you won't want the stage? What a thing to arrange, Anna!"

"I didn't arrange it. It arranged itself. I said any other time but tomorrow, and there was no other time. Edmund is leaving for Nice the day after."

"But, Anna, there is no reason . . ."

"Anything can be a reason," said Madame, and it was true that in her hands it could.

Miss Ilse sighed. "Even if you won't be using it, there is still the cleaning, and the florists will be there, you know the children are having it decorated for you. It isn't as if it were anything important."

"It may be imporrtant for Lollie."

"You may even be rehearsing."

"Surely to God not then, *still*. But we may," said Madame, and she sighed and turned away from Miss Ilse and went to the table and stood looking down at Jan's face. "I'm glad Jan won't be here tomorrow," she said slowly.

Miss Ilse looked up. "Anna. What is wrong?"

"Everything is wrong," said Madame vehemently. "Everything!"

"*Now?*"

"Yes. Now!"

"But, Anna! Things can't be wrong *now*. It's too late for them to be wrong!" cried Miss Ilse.

"They are."

"*Anna!*"

"Yes, *Anna!*" mocked Madame bitterly. "That is what I have been saying oll day, oll this day. This is a terrible day, Ilse. Now at the eleventh minute I know that I, Anna Holbein, have made a mistake. And what am I to do?"

"But . . . what mistake, Anna?"

"It is that ballet of Hilda's. Ah, I wish I had never seen her!" cried Madame. "I listened to Felix, to Lion, when I should have trusted myself. I have never liked it. Never."

"Then . . . why . . . ?"

"I don't know why," said Madame wearily, and shut her eyes. "Don't ask me why. Because we oll, oll of us, do stupid things. I liked the dance of 'Peace' in it. I liked her 'Evocation.'"

"Then . . ."

"I still like them," said Madame. "But I know now it is wrong."

"But . . . if you liked it before . . ." argued Miss Ilse, "perhaps it is just that you are tired . . . depressed, Anna. You know you are easily depressed . . ."

Madame's eyes flew open. "It is *wrrong*, Ilse," she said

severely. "Don't you hear me? Ah, don't make me such a storrm in a teapot about accepting one little worrd! It is wrrong. *Wrrong!*"

"Then . . . what are you going to do?"

"I don't know."

She walked past Miss Ilse to the window, back to the desk, and then to the table, where she stood and looked down on Jan's still mask. "Tomorrow is an occasion, not?" she said. "I suppose, really, I have waited for it oll my life. Yes, that could be said, Ilse. Fifty years of worrk. Fifty years of success . . . and now!"

"But, Anna . . . You say, often, that you don't understand modern work . . ."

"Nonsense! I understand everything," said Madame. "Now is not the old days," she said slowly. "Then . . . for everything, everyone, there was something, someone, we could put in its place. We had a repertoire. The company was experienced, more or less, but now . . . they are young, untried. I think I have worked too quickly. That is what comes of fitting your work to an occasion, Ilse. And so . . ." said Madame. "Now"—she made a helpless gesture with her hands—"if I cut it, I have no alternative . . . that I care to give, and I have no alternative . . . but to cut it," said Madame.

"If you cut it . . . you will *have* to put something in its place."

"Don't be a fool, Ilse," said Madame tersely. "Send Hilda to me."

"Anna . . . the poor child . . ." Miss Ilse had an inexplicable liking for Hilda, inexplicable to Madame. Hilda, from the first time Madame saw her, had always made her think of a little snake.

Madame Holbein had a propensity for likening her pupils to animals. In an atmosphere where personalities ran high, each was likely to find himself with two, his own and the one Madame had given him. It was in her class that Lion had first become Lion. "And Caroline must be a lamb, an ewe lamb." It was Hilda who said that, slit-tongued Hilda. Some of Madame's names were cruel but all of them were apt: Francis, who was inclined to be stout and pallid and who had pink-rimmed eyes, was a polar bear; Lao-Erh, the Anglo-Chinese child, with her neat eye, smooth head, and broad foot, was a Mandarin duck; John, easily startled, with great eyes and the thin long strength of his legs, was a gazelle; the handsome well-dressed flashy eleven-year-old Zoë was a jaguar, and Archie, both in looks and manners, was a street sparrow.

As if this were catching, Madame herself was like nothing so much as a little foreign monkey, sad in the English climate. If she were tired or excited, and she usually was tired or excited, she shivered and she huddled her purple woollen coat round her like a monkey's jacket. She was thin and small and light and agile and she had beautiful nutshell-shaped eyes, but, if they had a monkey sadness and sharpness, they were not shallow as a monkey's are; they were full of comprehension, sensitive and expressive; as

Madame grew older, more and more of her seemed to go into her eyes; and to her students, most of whom were bounded by their teens, Madame was very old indeed.

"Anna, you should retire. You burn yourself out. Surely you have enough of money and prestige?"

"It isn't the money," said Madame. "It isn't the prestige."

"But you are getting older, more frail. You get so tired, Anna."

"Yes. I get tired," admitted Madame.

"A little house, not this great barracks," said Miss Ilse longingly. "Think, you and I, sitting quietly by our own fire!"

"We can sit quietly when we are dead," said Madame. "I hope I shall work until I die."

The school at Holbein's existed for the theatre. "And not the theatre for the school," said Madame sharply to each pupil. "Don't you think it. It is not to be your lazy way in. They use me," said Madame. "What am I but a sprringboard, yes, a springboard, for their careers." No pupil who had passed through her school and company was more implacably bent on using her than Hilda.

Between Madame and everyone she taught was a direct strong personal link; too personal, her critics said. Pupils had either to be in entire submission or in conflict. Hilda was doomed to be in perpetual conflict.

Madame felt Hilda was a snake . . . or something to do with a snake . . . is it Eve? thought Madame. But we have no proof that Eve was an Egyptian. But what am I thinking? asked Madame. It was Felix who said that and not I. . . . The girl was not pretty, though she had a beautiful slender body, exceptional legs, straight and strong, and feet, long but finishing squarely, the toes remarkably even. "A dancer's foot," Madame might have said, but, for some reason, she grudged saying it. "She is like a snake," said Madame, and that was almost all she ever said of Hilda. It was true that Hilda's neck was a little long and that made her small wedge-shaped face look smaller; her hair was sandy brown and thick and fine, spread like a hood in small crinkled waves down to her neck. She had a very white skin: "One of those skins that do not change," said Madame. "They are insensitive." She liked the apple-blossom cheeks of the little Russian, Liuba Rayevskaya, or Caroline's fair colouring. "But Caroline has a beautiful complexion," said Madame. Hilda's eyes were green, faintly slanted; their lids were unusual; the lids were white and heavy and showed their veins in pale-blue markings, hyacinth-blue. If her skin were not sensitive, those eyelids were, but Madame did not look at them.

"Why don't you like her better?" said Miss Ilse.

"I don't like her at all."

"She is talented. Very talented."

"Yes," said Madame. "But . . . her talent is too strong."

"Can talent be too strong?"

Madame did not know the answer to that herself. Hilda puzzled her. She did not know the answer to Hilda.

The list of names of past pupils at Holbein's was illustrious; none of them as illustrious as Madame herself, but illustrious enough.

"But no one is illustrious now," said Madame. "No one. They have forgotten how to be."

"But, Anna, surely . . ."

"They are oll geese," said Madame fiercely.

"But, Anna, some of the children are good."

"Good! What good is good to me?" said Madame.

"I can tell you some names," said Miss Ilse. "Bianca. Michel Boré. Sonia Volskaya. Claudie. The little Lointaine . . ."

"They are oll gone," interrupted Madame.

"There will be more. There always are."

"Where? Where? Show them to me. In oll my life," said Madame, "I have never come across these children, these young girls, who dance by themselves in a passage or the moonlight and you are strruck dumb. I have never been struck dumb," said Madame. "No. Nonsense. Genius, if there *is* any genius, will discover itself by harrd worrk in its proper place in class. I have had no geniuses," said Madame.

There were too many names. Madame felt there were too many names, but at the same time she felt, as she felt today, that there were not enough. "Because look at what happens to them," said Madame. "Where are they now? Look at Bianca, what she is doing, and who can blame her?" Though Madame blamed her bitterly. Bianca was in Hollywood. "I do not teach for films and musicals," said Madame, but, often, that was where her teaching went. "Claudie has married and left the stage. Michel has grown fat . . ."

"Plump," pleaded Miss Ilse, who had liked Michel.

"Fat," said Madame. "Well, he is in New York now again, so I do not know how fat he is," she conceded. "He is in New York, and so is Sonia. I never see them now. So many go to America," said Madame.

"They dance just as well in America, Anna."

"And Lointaine is in Paris and I never see her either. Paul is back in Russia. Stephen and Edith in Australia."

"All over the world," said Miss Ilse.

"Yes, oll over the worrld," said Madame more cheerfully. She liked to think of that. She often talked of it. "I could paper the walls of the office with the stamps on the letters I have had from abroad this year," said Madame.

"Paper the walls with stamps!" said the literal Lollie Porteus. She worked it out. Allowing for the window and the door and the fireplace, the answer came to one hundred and thirteen thousand, four hundred stamps. "Would even Madame have that many letters in a year?" asked Lollie, but her faith in Madame was unshaken.

It was true that dancers from the Holbein Ballet covered the world. "And you can say they are pedigree dancers," said Madame. "They have been taught by me and I was taught by Marli and Galina Shumskaya herself. I, a pupil of Shumskaya, who was a pupil of Semyenova who was a pupil of Krassouskaya. We are in dirrect tradition. Yes. There are not many like me," said Madame, "and I was not fit to kiss her hand," she said reverently of Marli. "She was verry great artist."

Now she had only this handful of young ones in the school, "and only a school, not a company," said Madame. "We have never been so young, so without experience." Over and over again she would go over their names. "John. Liuba. Yes, Liubochka does very well, but . . . no more than that . . ." said Madame with a sigh. Liuba Rayevskaya was to dance the Eldest Pupil in *Cat Among the Pigeons*, with John as the Interloper. "I am giving them their chance," said Madame. She had hesitated between Rayevskaya and Hilda, but she had finally given Hilda the second part, the Second Pupil, and cast her as the Waiting Maid, second to Caroline, in the last ballet on the programme, *The Noble Life*.

"Then Hilda is not to have anything?" asked Miss Ilse.

"What do you mean, anything? She has two good parts."

"They are not good enough for Hilda," said Miss Ilse, with unaccustomed boldness. "Felix thinks so too."

"Felix can keep his nose out of the pie," said Madame.

"And so does Lion."

"What does Lion know? A boy like that?"

"He isn't a boy. He is a young man. You allow him to help you with rehearsals, more than Rebecca," said Miss Ilse.

"Because he helps more than Rebecca, and that is for his sake, not for mine," said Madame coldly. "I am teaching him," said Madame.

No one, not even Miss Ilse, knew what would induce Madame to take one pupil, or refuse another. Perhaps she did not always know herself. Some that appeared promising, she refused; others, for no apparent reason, she took. It was the same with the fees. "They should pay me hundreds of pounds," said Madame. "For what I teach them they should pay hundreds of pounds." Then she would take someone, like Lollie, for nothing.

Lion had been taken for nothing. Years ago he had come by himself and rung the bell and waited two hours outside the door for an answer. And it was winter, said Madame. What a little gamin he was! An arab from the street, dirty, thin, a ragged little boy. Now he had grown to this immense black-haired gold-skinned young man, muscular, lean, with wide shoulders, narrow-hipped and beautiful. . . . I look at you sometimes, thought Madame, and I don't know where you come from! . . . He was now with Caroline in the Metropolitan Theatre Company. Very often they were cast as partners. Caroline and Lion were Madame's two almost-realized hopes. From her first lesson, Caroline had begun to make a career for herself.

"She had an easy way in," said Miss Ilse. "She has rich parents who give her all she wants."

"That can make no difference to her dancing."

"It can make her path smooth. She has never had to struggle. One day . . ."

"One day I shall show her to Gustave," said Madame dreamily. "Ilse. I have heard that Gustave is in London.

Then why hasn't he come? Does he think I have no one now to show him? But one day I shall show him Lion and Caroline."

The students in the school called Lion "Golden-Syrup Lion" from the lion that was a trade-mark on the tin of a certain brand of golden syrup. Madame when she heard it was indignant.

"It is right," said Mr. Felix. "He is too sweet. He agrees with every word you say."

"Lion has sense," said Madame. "Naturally he agrees with me. He knows where I can help him."

"He knows too well. Still . . . he may turn out all right," said Mr. Felix, "but I should watch Caroline. She has sharp elbows."

"It is my plan," said Madame, disregarding him, "that Lion shall have this company when I die, he . . . and Caroline."

"H'mm!" said Mr. Felix.

"Caroline has great personal beauty," said Madame, up in arms. "You can't deny it."

"I don't deny it. I don't like it," said Mr. Felix, and he added, "I have never thought a great deal of Caroline."

"Then you are mistaken."

"So may you be," said Mr. Felix. "Even you."

It was said in the school that Mr. Felix had once upon a time been a concert pianist. Mr. Felix did not say it. He had been musical director of the little Holbein Theatre since it had started and before that been with Madame on her tours and had often acted as her accompanist. He was a small old man with sparse white silky hair; his skin was the colour of yellowed ivory; he was Tartar in physiognomy and had blue eyes as bright as forget-me-nots. He played with dexterity, considering he had lost the tops of three fingers of his right hand. "Considering that, not otherwise," said Mr. Felix.

He played for such of Madame's classes as had music with perfect accuracy, while he read a book propped up in front of him on the music rack. Miss Ilse felt this was rude and tried to remonstrate with him. "You are playing for the children. You should watch them."

"I should if there were anything to watch."

"The mothers don't like it."

"I am not playing for the mothers. I am playing for the children, you just said so."

The book was usually a history book, but not always. "I find history, equally, in a novel," said Mr. Felix. He might have said he found history, equally, in everything and everyone.

"My world should have been music," said Mr. Felix. "But, as that has been prevented, meaning my fingers, the dance does nicely instead; quite nicely, that is." With any-one else, his pause would have been a sigh. "It is more ob-vious, more poignant, more exciting, and more easy to understand, and, perhaps, it suits me better," said Mr. Felix, "because I am growing old; not nerve-old, excitable-old, like Anna, but bone-old, and I don't want to bother

too much. I study this little world," said Mr. Felix. "It has
life, death, history, and, like any other world, it turns, unconsidered among other worlds, or almost unconsidered because it is a little famous. . . ." He chuckled. "They think
I detach myself from my history book to consider it, but,
of course, I don't. It and my history book are exactly the
same."

"What would you have done, Mr. Felix, if your fingers
had been taken off a little shorter," asked Archie, "so that
you couldn't have played the piano at all?"

"I should have been a taxi-driver," said Mr. Felix, "and
driven about in my taxi and watched the world from my
little seat as I do now."

It was Mr. Felix, more than Lion, who had made Madame direct her attention to Hilda. Madame knew that Lion
often danced through these ballets of Hilda's with her, and
criticized and helped her. Lion was attracted by Hilda,
Madame knew that too and did not want to know it; but
Mr. Felix had no reason for praising Hilda except that he
thought her worth his praise, "And Felix knows more about
dancers than most people have forgotten," said Madame.
It seemed that her attention was directed to Hilda, willy-
nilly.

Now she said suddenly, "Do you remember, Ilse, when
the children gave me the Fête on my birthday, do you remember that *Guy* of Hilda's? Do you remember how clever
Felix thought it was?"

"It was clever," said Miss Ilse. "It was horrible. I hated it.

I remember wishing I need not see an uncomfortable dance like that. It was a little *Petrouchka*."

"It wasn't *Petrouchka*," said Madame. "It wasn't anything but itself. It had its own flavour. It was original. Something good ought to have come from that child." She looked at the clock. "We have only a few minutes before rehearsal. I must make up my mind." She sighed and beat her hands together, one into the palm of the other, in distress. "Don't stand there staring at me, Ilse. Send Hilda to me."

When Hilda came she was not made up but her hair was done in the coils and satin bow of the Second Pupil; she was in tights and her practice dress and she was breathing quickly. "I was . . . warming up," she said breathlessly. Madame could see she was in a glow of excitement. Well, I olways was, thought Madame involuntarily. Each time. Yes. I was arrdent, thought Madame. So is she. . . . But she smothered that thought and returned to the worry over the ballet and her voice was crisp and cold as she said, "Hilda, I have sent for you because I am not satisfied with your *Lyre*."

Hilda's eyes widened in astonishment. "But . . . I thought . . ."

"Never mind what you thought," said Madame. She did not know why she spoke so cruelly. Hilda's lids fell and her face grew hard.

"I need not tell you, Hilda," said Madame, "that it is quite extraordinary for so young and inexperienced a choreographer—though you are not yet a choreographer, of course—for so young a girl, then, to be allowed to prroduce her worrk on an occasion like tomorrow." Madame did not know herself why she was making this long preamble; she was not given to speeches. "I think I can say that my anniversary is uncommon. It is unique. Isn't it unique, Hilda?"

"Yes, Madame." Hilda hardly opened her lips. *She isn't thinking of me at oll*, thought Madame with irritation. *She is thinking of herself!* "It is a chance for you," said Madame severely. "An enormous chance. A girl of only seventeen . . . I ask you?"

But she isn't seventeen, thought Madame irritably. *She is as old as the hills. I hate hills*, thought Madame. *Baffling and steep. Spoiling the view. No good is going to come out of this*, said Madame.

She remembered when she had first discussed the ballet with Hilda, how obstinate she had been and how she, Madame, had then a feeling of acting against her better judgment. *I ought to have waited, talked to her, encouraged her to write something else, been* sympathetic, thought Madame, but she could not tell, even now, how she could have brought herself to be sympathetic to Hilda. "Either you are, or you are not," said Madame. "It is no good disguising it, not?"

"Well, what is this ballet?" she had said then. "Tell it to me. Tell it."

"It is called *Lyre with Seven Strings*."

"It isn't Greek, or Chinese, or Irish?" asked Madame with suspicion.

Hilda said distantly that it had no country. "There is Man. Universal Man. You could call him Adam . . . or John Smith."

"Ah! One of those!" said Madame. "Ah well! Well, go on."

Hilda explained that she had taken the idea from a novel of George Sand. She thought that George Sand had taken the idea from . . . "But why does that matter?" interrupted Madame. "It doesn't matter where you got it from, it matters what it is. Well, what is it? Go on."

Man's aspiration was like the lyre, Hilda explained seriously, and he could attain to harmony only after he had learnt to play on all the seven strings.

"Nonsense!" said Madame. "You can have harmony with two or three or four."

"Not full harmony," said Hilda. In the ballet, the strings were dancers who embodied their qualities. "Man dances with each in turn," said Hilda. "The strings are Peace, War, Sorrow, Joy, Evocation, Love, and God."

"You can't have God in a ballet," said Madame.

Hilda explained that when it came to God, Man danced by himself, alone.

"Then how does one know it is God?"

It was certainly hard to tell it to Madame. Hilda found herself wishing that she had chosen something more simple.

"I have the synopsis here, and my notes," she said, and,

in spite of herself, her hurt dignity showed in her voice. Madame looked up. She knew how much work and earnestness Hilda had put into this ballet and she curbed her tongue. "Let me look at them," she said, and she gave Hilda the recognition of looking at them carefully. "It is an idea," she said slowly. "Well, I should like to see some of it, one or two of the dances. . . ."

Hilda's lids flew up and her eyes shone with faith and hope. "Would you?" she said. Now her voice is like an ordinary young girl's, thought Madame. She looked at Hilda and she had a sudden and surprising pang of jealousy. Hilda's green eyes were incandescently pure. That is because she is young . . . and untouched, said Madame. My eyes are far more beautiful than hers, even now, said Madame, but they can never look like that because I am old and she is young. . . . Suddenly she hated Hilda for being young.

"What is your music?" she said, and she added sarcastically, "Scriabin?"

Hilda said with dignity that it was not Scriabin, it was Zedek.

"I never heard of him."

A smile flickered at the corners of Hilda's mouth. "He is a contemporary Czech composer," she said gently, but Madame had seen the smile and she did not forgive her.

"Mr. Felix helped you with that."

"No," said Hilda truthfully. Mr. Felix had refused to help her. "If you want to find out music you must find it out for yourself. That will teach you!" said Mr. Felix, though whether he meant it as a threat or a fact Hilda did not know. "If you want to do these ballets, do them by yourself," said Mr. Felix to her later. "Don't let anyone else lay a finger on them."

"I only want advice."

"Advice is the worst kind of help. It is pernicious, and if you don't know what that means," said Mr. Felix, "you should go and look it up in the dictionary." Hilda looked it up and was surprised to find how strong and final its meaning was.

"Once . . . I showed him some music . . ." She hesitated and said, "It was recorded. I found it and showed it to him. He said he thought it should make a good ballet. That was a year ago but I couldn't forget it, and . . ."

"Is there anyone here who knows this? Who has danced any of it?" interrupted Madame. She had not been listening.

"John and Alma know it, and Francis, and Liuba. They are here. I can fetch them in a minute. They will come. I have the records."

It was all arranged promptly. It is surprising how obliging they are when it is something they want, thought Madame.

She did not like the theme. If life were to be a lyre, she thought, its strings, life's attributes, it was her experience that you did not learn to play them one by one as you were ready, but . . . higgledy-piggledy, thought Madame, willy-nilly. . . . Hilda knew better. The ballet was perfectly clear, unusually well arranged. Madame immediately liked the dance of "Peace," with Adam, or John Smith; in Hilda's "Peace," the usual roles were reversed and it was the female partner who was the background for the male, who kept the sustaining part; and what surprised Madame was the restraint of its whole conception . . . that is unusual in the work of so young a girl. . . . She did not like "Sorrow," nor "War"; "they are gloomy, heavy." Hilda said she thought they should be gloomy and heavy; after all, she pointed out, they were Sorrow and War. "They are overdone," said Madame. "Sometimes you are too strong, in everything. Why, when you have that restraint? Sometimes you overdance." Hilda did not understand that herself. "It's because you are young," said Madame.

Neither did Madame like "Love." "It is dull and flat and staid," she said. "You had it coming. It was good to begin with, but it should have gone quicker, quicker, quicker, more fast, and then he should have swept her up and taken her away. Not go back to the firrst rhythm like that."

"But that . . . that you are thinking of," said Hilda, "is only one aspect of love. I want to show it all."

"My dearr child! Who are you?" said Madame, and she returned to the argument. "It gets tedious. You should *not* go back to the first theme like that."

"The music does."

"But love doesn't."

"The music does."

"Then change the music."

Hilda answered with austerity that she did not think *she* should change the music.

"But you *should*," said Madame. "You should change it and chop it and twist it and do anything with it rather than spoil your ballet. I olways did," said Madame.

Hilda was superiorly silent. What a little prrig she is, thought Madame, and then "Evocation" made her smile. "I said you had wit, Hilda," she cried. "This is delightful." When Hilda saw that smile she knew that she had succeeded, though, for a long time, it was to be a mystery to Hilda that she, who was so deadly serious about her work— "Yes, deadly," said Madame—should be able to make people smile with scarcely an effort; and still more mysterious why Madame and, later on, other people for whose opinion she had the deepest respect should think that far more clever than her serious work. It would take years for Hilda to discover that it was her serious work.

"You will write a real ballet one day," said Madame when she had seen *Lyre with Seven Strings* through. Hilda did not know whether to be proud or offended.

"But . . . is it good?" she asked. She always remembered Madame's answer.

"Why should it be good?" said Madame. "Think what it takes to make something good, what brrains and knowledge and experience. Who are you? You are oll the same, you young ones. Is it good? You should thank God you can do it at oll."

Hilda still wanted to know if it were good. Now she had

to stand before Madame in the office and wait for her to continue this laceration.

"I am sorry I have to tell you this," said Madame. "I blame myself. I don't know where my eyes have been, and my ears, oll my five wits. We must be frank, Hilda, not? This is the truth. I have made a mistake."

"A mistake?" Small white patches showed round Hilda's nostrils, her voice was tight, otherwise she showed no emotion at all.

"We shall have to cut it," said Madame.

Hilda said nothing but Madame could see the breast of her tunic rising tempestuously up and down as she breathed, and she could see a quiver in her throat. But that is only muscles, said Madame scornfully. People should show feeling in their eyes.

"I shall have to cut it," said Madame aloud, "unless . . ."

Hilda's lids flicked up, flicked down. There was a knock on the door and Mr. Felix came in with Lion. Now Hilda felt as if she were facing an inquisition. She did not know which side Mr. Felix was on, if he were on any side; in his brown alpaca coat, with his silky hair brushing his coat collar, he looked a mild old man far removed from this torture, but she felt he would watch gravely to see how she behaved under it. She did not look at Lion but she was acutely aware that he was there.

"I am telling Hilda I am afraid we must cut *Lyre*."

They all looked at Hilda. She kept her lids down but she knew they must guess she was pressing back tears. Tears would be natural, thought Madame. It would be natural to storm and to cry. It is a disappointment, but you will see. She won't shed a tear. She is sly.

"Cut it? Altogether?" asked Lion, his eyes bright with pity and interest. "All of it?"

Mr. Felix said nothing. He waited.

"Perhaps I need not do that," said Madame slowly. "I have wondered if we couldn't make of it a suite of dances." Hilda's head came up sharply and her eyes opened, looking at Madame with even more astonishment. "A suite of dances," repeated Madame. "We could call them *Meditations* or something like that. *Meditations on the Qualities,* not? We should keep four, I think. 'Peace,' 'Joy,' 'Evocation,' and 'Love' . . . 'Love' with my alterations, of course, yes?"

"No," said Hilda.

There was silence.

"Do you say 'No' to me, Hilda?"

Hilda's eyes were level with Madame's. Now Madame could not have said she looked sly. She looked desperate and defiant. "It won't be my ballet," said Hilda.

"It will be a good deal better than your ballet."

"It will be founded on yours. In fact it will be all yours," said Lion.

Hilda only said again, "It won't be my ballet."

"It will be the best part, with the worst cut away," said Lion. "The dances Madame has chosen *are* the best, and they won't be spoilt by the faults of the others."

Hilda looked past him to Madame. "Isn't it better to have your own faults?" asked Hilda, and Madame knew she was right.

Cut it. Throw it out. Be cruel. Execrate it, misjudge it, but don't persuade her to change it against her will, said something in Madame. . . . As far as it is in her power she has made it complete. If she has no more power that is a pity, but it is none the less complete. Then take it or leave it, said Madame silently to herself. But . . . surely she must be guided, said a second part of Madame. Why should she produce a faulty thing on my stage? . . . Again she contradicted that with the feeling that it would be better to have it faulty than interfere. . . . But I should be ashamed for them to see it, said Madame. What does that matter? her first part said steadily, refusing to be moved. What does that matter? They are lucky to see it at all, if it is interesting. It is the thing she is trying to do that matters, not they . . . the audience. But you can't have ballet without an audience, cried Madame. If I put on ballets like this I should soon have no audience at oll. One must be expedient. . . . She caught herself up. That was a word she had blamed other people for using and said she should never consent to use herself. The word seemed to hang on the air and its after-taste was sour. . . . Words don't have tastes, said Madame, but she felt its sourness and, beginning to be angry, she tapped her foot impatiently and said, "Well, Hilda?"

Hilda could not answer.

Why am I doing this? Madame asked herself. To make up my programme, not because I sincerely believe that, in this form, her ballet will be good. It is good olready, as good as ever it will be; that is, it has the elements of being good. . . . She paused, puzzled herself to know what to say next.

"I like it better like this," said Lion. "I think it sounds terribly attractive."

"Terribly is surely the wrong word," murmured Mr. Felix.

"The dresses are made and the set," said Lion, "and, after all, Hilda, Madame has paid for them. I think you should think of that."

"I do think of it," said Hilda desperately.

"And think of all the work, Mr. Felix's, the company's, mine, and Madame's. Above all, hers. You are under an obligation to Madame Holbein, Hilda."

"She is under no obligation," said Madame coldly. "It's not her fault that I made a mistake."

"Hilda," said Lion with his extraordinary sweetness, "Madame must know better than you."

"Yes. I know, but . . ." said Hilda, trying to find words to defend herself.

"Then . . . ?"

"She doesn't know my ballet as I do. She . . . she can't." It was torn out of her and she knew it sounded young and crude. She turned from them in despair. They were all arraigned against her. She had no choice. Then she looked up and saw Mr. Felix watching her as if he thought she had a choice.

If one looks at the faces of most young girls, they have two halves to their faces; one shows what they are now, the other what they will become. Hilda had only one face and it was set, implacable as a little stone, on what she intended to do.

Long ago Madame could have placed her in one of the ballet companies. She could have gone to the Metropolitan last year. Madame's own Michel Boré on his tour from America had seen her and wanted to take her back with him but she would not go. "What more do you want?" Madame had asked her then.

"That isn't what I want," Hilda had answered and she had said, as if she were talking to herself, "I want more than that."

At Holbein's she was labelled conceited and yet, if one came to examine it, it was a queer conceit that kept her working month after month as a class pupil and nothing more. "Why don't you leave, Hilda?" Lion had urged her.

"I'm not ready to leave."

"But it's ridiculous. You need stage experience, no matter what you want to do."

Hilda shook her head. "Not that stage experience," she said, and, as she looked past him, he thought she saw further than he did. "Where else should I find a possible stage?" asked Hilda.

"Possible?" asked Lion puzzled.

"Possible for me," said Hilda.

Now Hilda was attracted from her path. Lion had drawn her aside and was talking to her, earnestly and quietly, his head bent down close to hers. Madame watched them.

"A lion should have a mane," said Mr. Felix, and Madame saw that Lion's head with its shorn black curls was more like a ram than a lion. A sheep! thought Madame, and caught the thought back, and looked daggers at Mr. Felix.

As Hilda looked up at Lion, Madame saw colour steal slowly up her cheeks. She couldn't blush outright, said Madame. No. She isn't honest enough for that, but she blushes oll the same. It gave Madame a feeling of triumph that Hilda, the superior Hilda, was like any other girl. The same, just the same, said Madame. She was spiteful because she was jealous. "Go and talk it over with Lion," said Madame aloud. "You have a few minutes before rehearsal. Talk it over with Lion," said Madame treacherously.

As she said it, she knew that she knew of a better way; that there was something altogether different, adult and inspired, that she could have said to Hilda to help her, and that no one else but she, Madame, could say . . . because no one else has the knowledge, said Madame; but this second, wilful, jealous, petty part in her would not let it be said. And so, I throw Hilda to the lions, she thought, but she did not laugh. She saw Mr. Felix give her a stern glance. Felix is olways poking his nose in my pie, she thought crossly, and was all the crosser when she remembered that it was she who had asked him to be there. Together they watched while Lion, his hand under Hilda's elbow, took her, still talking earnestly, to the door. Hilda went with him as if mesmerized. And who shall blame her? said Madame with a pang in her heart. Isn't he oll he should be? Big, attractive, gay and sweet and kind? But, she thought involuntarily, he should be more than that. . . . What made her think it? She did not know. Then Hilda, who was at the door, released herself brusquely and turned round and came back to Madame.

Ah, she is like me! thought Madame. At the eleventh minute she saves herself, not? . . . She saw it with admiration but with irritation as well.

Hilda had lost her tinge of colour. She was as pale as ever and her eyes were wide and distraught with unhappiness. "I can't agree," said Hilda. "Madame. I'm sorry, but I can't. I know what you all think and I expect you are right, but . . . you must have it as it is, or not at all."

She stood, her eyes on Madame beseeching her to understand.

"You are arrogant and conceited," said Madame, as she would have killed a fly. "Then . . . not at oll." And she walked out of the office.

Outside the door she almost stepped on a small girl who, instead of backing away, stayed where she was.

"What do you want, Lollie? Who told you to come upstairs? What are you doing up here in my prrivate hall?"

"You sent for me," said Lollie calmly.

She had been in the hall for quite a long time, but she did not mind that. The floor of the hall was in black-and-white marble squares, cool and polished. Lollie remembered the first time she had seen them. "Marble? Is it *real* marble?" she had asked, and tiptoed across it as if her tread might crack it. She liked to be alone with its opulence. Lollie had a capacity for reverence, but not even Madame could have called her a chameleon. For instance, she reverenced Madame but, as Madame had already noticed, she remained firm.

"*Lollie!*" cried Madame when she had first come. "No one is called Lollie."

"I am."

"But it isn't a name."

"It is my name."

It was not her name. She did not intend to tell Madame her name, because she very justly thought that if Madame knew it, she would approve of it and use it. Lollie's name was Ingeborg. It would be years before she would come to appreciate it.

"Now how does Miss Porteus, with her red eyes and her thin bent shoulders and her sniffles and her arthritis, come to have a niece like that?" asked Madame.

"Backgrounds don't matter here." Madame said that often, but it was not true, because every one of the dancers carried something of this background with him like a halo or an aura. Lollie was a refreshing child with an antiquated staid little turn of speech that made people smile though she said nothing that was funny; she had what Madame called a two-edged smile, that sprang joyfully to her eyes while it was woe-begone and curiously touching on her lips. "With a smile like that she is made," said Rebecca. "Even without her dancing." She had a fine slender small physique with the promise of what Madame said might be classical beauty, and she was remarkably gifted, but she showed very clearly the poverty of her upbringing and background, not only in food and clothes and language and knowledge but in ideas.

"Your horizon is no bigger than this saucer," Madame told her once, but Lollie did not even know, then, what a horizon was. Holbein's was making it larger. "I have been moved up in school," she told Madame. "I am learning music now as you said." It was Madame who was paying for the lessons. "And I know the names of the stars."

"What stars? What sort of stars?" asked Madame suspiciously.

"Aldebaran and Sirius and those."

"Six months ago you would have meant film stars."

Madame remembered coming on Lollie standing ignominiously outside the door of Rebecca's class. "She told me to be the wind in a field of corn," said Lollie. "How could I be? I have never seen a field of corn."

So much of my dancing, said Madame, came out of my childhood. . . . Her childhood had been spent in her grandmother's house in the country, or travelling with Jan. . . . At Lollie's age . . . thought Madame, and sighed.

However gifted she might be, no one could make that difference up in Lollie.

For everyone there is someone for whom, with whom, they cannot do wrong. Madame was fallible, but she was infallible for Lollie, as she had been for Lion. From the beginning, as she had with him, Madame taught Lollie far more than dancing. She allowed Lollie to talk to her as she allowed none of the others. "They do not need it," said Madame, "they have so much at home, but these lost children need me." They were, to her, lost in the immensity of the world they had to fight and they seemed to her to have no strength to borrow from but hers. She let Lollie be more intimate than the little Lion had been, because, in some curious way, Lollie seemed to her a reflection of herself.

Once Lollie had come to class with dirty finger-nails and Madame had execrated her. Lollie had borne it in silence but afterwards she told Madame that she did not see what finger-nails had to do with dancing. "Oll of you, every little bit, is to do with dancing," Madame had answered and she told Lollie how, long ago, Jan had said that to her.

"What did you say?" asked Lollie.

"I said it was going too far, and Jan said, 'Not nearly far enough. For you, everything you see and hear and touch and taste and smell is to do with dancing, *if* you are a dancer.'"

"If you are a dancer," repeated Lollie thoughtfully. She was not at all sure, at times, that she could be one. It was very arduous. It was only what Auntie called her obstinacy, an obstinate belief in her own dancing, that made her go steadily on.

Madame knew that, but even she did not know what a struggle it was.

Once Lollie had seen Miss Ilse cutting up a dried-looking fruit for Madame; when it was opened on the plate it showed myriads of deep red seeds. "What is it?" asked Lollie.

"A pomegranate. Those are its seeds."

"They look like blood."

"Yes. They call the Martyrs pomegranate seeds," said Miss Ilse absently. "The seed of the blood of the Church."

"What are martyrs?"

"You are a martyr if you believe and suffer for your faith. You can die for it."

"Oh, Saints!"

"Not only Saints. Everyone who believes must prepare to be a martyr more or less," said Madame, who had come in. "You believe you are going to be a dancer. Already you have to do for that, things that other children don't do; give up your playtime, work when you are tired. But you believe you will be a dancer and you must suffer for it."

Miss Ilse arranged the pieces of pomegranate on a Dresden plate and Madame carried them away.

Lollie was a martyr. A new child did not have an easy time among the other children at Holbein's. "They are fiends to one another. Perrfect little fiends," said Madame. She had no myopia about children; because they were small, she did not make excuses for them either as people or dancers; and as dancers, she did not give them any quarter though she knew that, like themselves, their scope was small.

With few exceptions, the orbit of a dancer moves entirely round himself, and the smaller he is, the lower down the scale, the more petty that orbit is. Each pupil in the Beginners' Class at Holbein's, Madame's "eggs" as she called them, "because we don't know what they will hatch into," looked on each new other one as a personal threat. Lollie was new and small but already she had ousted Zoë, the big showy child who was the leader of the class, and she had ousted Archie, who, up till then, had showed the greatest promise. Madame had given no sign of this but the class knew it to the last hair on their little bodies. The only person who did not know it was Lollie. The more Madame valued a pupil, the more she execrated him or her, but Lollie was not to know this, and she was bewildered by the criticisms that were poured on her head when she had obviously done the best *enchaînement* and listened to every word that Madame said.

Now she wondered miserably why she was sent for; though she appeared calm, Lollie's calmness was often the calmness of acceptance. It was no surprise to Lollie to be scolded any more than it was a surprise to be cold or tired or hungry. She had heard the angry voices in the office. It's a funny time to scold, thought Lollie, just before the big rehearsal . . . but she knew what she had done. It's the shoes, thought Lollie, and she burned wearily with guilt and shame.

Shoes were Auntie's and Lollie's nightmare. The shops for ballet shoes were in Soho or far away down the Charing Cross Road, and it was necessary to be there early and to queue for them and that meant being late for school. Lollie needed blocked shoes now, and unblocked shoes and heeled shoes for character dancing, and they were eight-and-six a pair. No matter how carefully she looked after them, they soon became dirty and worn.

"You must practise, Lollie. While you wait for your aunt and the rooms are empty, you must practise." Yes, but if she practised her shoes wore out. The others had mothers and fathers to buy their shoes for them, and so, when they had gone home, Lollie took their shoes out of their pigeon-holes and wore them to practise in and save her own.

"Lollie." Lollie looked up sharply, her eyes stretched with fear, her brow stretched too as if the bows of her turned-up plaits were tied too tightly.

"Why do you look so frightened?" asked Madame. "You look at me with eyes like a hare." Then she softened. Lollie, with her huge scared eyes, as expressive as Madame's own, and her hair strained back and plaited and turned up in bows like ears each side of her face, looked, not like a hare, but a very young caught leveret. "There is nothing to be frightened of," said Madame irritably. She sat down on a chest in the hall. "Lollie," she said, "will you grow up conceited and more clever than your olders? Yes, you will. You are sure to, and use me like a . . . like a cat's paw," said Madame.

"Pardon?" said Lollie politely, and looked so frightened that Madame had to laugh. She laughed unwillingly. There. You see, she thought. I can't even be angry in peace. She remembered now why she had sent for Lollie.

"You have never danced on the stage, have you, Lollie?"

"Yes, I have," said Lollie. (Then it was not the shoes.) "I have danced at the Coliseum, in matinees, twice. I was the Seed Pearl in the *Under-the-Water* ballet, and next time I was a Half Pint of Milk. I wore white for both."

"I see," said Madame. "Did you like it?"

"No," said Lollie. "That is one of my troubles. I get stage fright."

"Every dancer, that is worrth anything, olways gets stage fright."

"Doesn't she . . . *ever* get over it?" asked Lollie faintly.

"Never. The greater she is, probably the more she is nervous and strung up, because more is expected of her. She will be in a state of nerves, each time she waits to dance."

"*Each* time?"

"Each time," said Madame firmly.

"Well, I'm too young to get a licence," said Lollie comfortably. "My cousin was in *Puss in Boots* at Croydon last Christmas."

"You have no need to dance in Pantomime," said Madame.

"Three pounds a week," said Lollie, and sighed.

"You have other things to do," said Madame. "Now listen to me. You have worked well this year and I am pleased with you, though I should be more pleased," said Madame with a sudden riposte, "if I had not had to see that *cabriole* you showed me this morning, or what you called a *cabriole*, from the *Arabesque: jeté, glissé, pas de chat,* and off with the *cabriole*. Remember?" Lollie winced and hung her head. She remembered.

"But still, I am pleased with you and I have decided to give you a chance. It will please your auntie, not? It happens that a friend of mine, Mr. Edmund White, of Broadwood Studios, is looking for a child dancer, not for very much, you understand, but to appear and dance in his new film. It is the life of a ballerina, or what they think is the life of a ballerina," said Madame severely. "He has asked me to find him such a child and I have thought of you."

"Me!" cried Lollie aghast.

"Say 'I,' not 'me,' Lollie."

"I? I couldn't do that," said Lollie decidedly.

"You will have to pass a test, of course." Madame went on as if she had not heard her. "A screen test, but first Mr. White will give you an audition. He is coming here, to the theatre at four o'clock tomorrow . . ."

"But, Madame . . ."

"Lollie!" Madame fixed her with a stern eye and Lollie quailed.

"What . . . what shall I dance?" she said weakly.

Madame thought. "The variation I taught you in class. You know that well."

"But . . . it's not even a dance," said Lollie. "Couldn't I do my Polish dance and wear my Polish dress?" The Polish dance was difficult but Lollie mysteriously knew it would be easier to dance at an audition than the variation. Madame took that hope from her.

"No. In a character dance you will be that character, that is if you dance it as you should, which you don't olways, Lollie. He will want to see you as you are. You will dance the variation."

The prelude that accompanied the variation immediately began in Lollie's head, but instead of the steps that went to it she found she was thinking of those she had been wrong in that morning! From the *Arabesque: jeté, glissé, pas de chat*, then off with the *cabriole*. But that isn't it at all, thought Lollie, and she looked at Madame in despair. "I shall never do it," said Lollie.

"You must."

"But . . . I am no good at auditions," said Lollie with conviction.

"You have been prroperly taught. You have only to keep your head," said Madame unsympathetically.

"But . . ."

"Then you would like me to give it to Zoë? Or perhaps to little Miette?"

Lollie flushed. She had suffered from Zoë, and Miette was the newest and youngest and latest joined.

"You cannot have it every way, Lollie. You must choose. Perhaps you would rather be a dressmaker, say, like your aunt?" Then suddenly Madame softened. "Auditions are nothing to be afraid of, any more than a bridge," she said. "They are a means of travelling, that is oll. If you get this parrt, if you don't get it, makes no difference to your dancing, it doesn't matter, but what *does* matter," said Madame severely, "is if you dance well."

"Yes, Madame."

"It is like photographs. Do I mind being photographed, I ask you? It is tiresome, yes, but it is my duty and you must learn what your duty is. The imporrtant thing is . . . Is the pose natural and beautiful as it should be in the dance? I olways photograph perrfectly," said Madame.

"Yes, Madame," said Lollie.

"*Or* an examination. What is an examination? A little stick to measure your technique. Naturally you pass them, coming from here, but they don't mean that you can dance. Ah, dearr no!" said Madame, getting up from the chest. "Now don't let me waste my breath on air, Lollie."

"No, Madame."

Chassée, arabesque, assemblée over, *jeté croisée,* repeat, thought Lollie. That was it, but then she was back again: From the *Arabesque: jeté, glissé, pas de chat,* off with the *cabriole.* What shall I do if I go off with the *cabriole* in the middle? thought Lollie. And what shall I wear? . . . Her tutu was too short, there was no time for Auntie to make her a new one, and her tunics were darned and old. Lollie had heard enough about auditions to know that one should look attractive, as attractive as one could, but tomorrow was the Opening and no one, Lollie knew very certainly, would have a minute to spare for her. The-Opening-old-darned-tunic-*pas-de-chat-cabriole*, thought Lollie, in the snare.

"Madame . . ."

"What *is* it, Lollie?"

Lollie had not the courage to say what it was; she said instead, "Madame, will . . . you be there?"

Madame paused, looked down at her. "Do you want me to be there?" Lollie nodded. She could not speak, but at that moment, however sharp Madame might be afterwards, she wanted Madame to be there.

"Your teacher can't hold your hand for ever," said Madame, "but I shall be there, I promise you. Now don't look so frightened. A promise is a promise, not? . . .

"And now where is everyone?" cried Madame. "We are late. Everyone is late. Felix. Lion. Is no one here? Where are oll the children? And Rebecca? And Miss Parkes. Ilse? You are never here when I want you. Are we to stand about oll evening? There you are, Miss Parkes. Here I have been standing for hours and hours . . . Is my time nothing? Ah, in the theatre? Why didn't you say so before? Go and tell them I am coming. We must go thrrough everything, not run through, but completely. What hours I wait and no one is ready for me yet!"

Lollie was left standing in the hall.

Madame had to have an audition before she passed into the Imperial School, thought Lollie. She had often heard her tell of that. "So many judges," said Madame, "the management, the teachers, past and present dancers, some famous names, famous even to me, that ignorrant little girl. There were more than a hundred candidates and they oll seemed to me so beautiful and strrong and prrettily dressed, and I had only a small old pale-blue dress that Jan had borrowed for me; we were very poor then, very poor. What chance had I?" said Madame dramatically, "a small pale girl among so many? How wise and clever those judges must have been to see such prromise in her."

Will they see mine in me? asked Lollie bitterly. Me in my old white tunic. She decided they would not and stood, frowning at the marble squares to think what she should do. Madame ought to have known, thought Lollie.

Perhaps Madame was right to overlook the difficulties. Difficulties can be surmounted and they are no excuse.

"Well, you have lost an opportunity," said Lion.

"I know," said Hilda in a tense, proud little voice, and turned her back on him and walked to the window.

When Madame left the office Hilda had walked out after her and blindly past her and Lollie and into the classroom.

"H'm!" said Mr. Felix, and wiped his forehead on his handkerchief. Mr. Felix's handkerchiefs were like himself, thin, old, yellowed, but of a good quality, but Lion did not look at it but at Mr. Felix. Mr. Felix looked as if for once he really cared, and he looked satisfied.

"What a little fool!" said Lion.

"Yes. You can't please God and Mammon," said Mr. Felix politely.

Lion glared at him, hesitated, and went out after Hilda.

He was genuinely astonished at Hilda, astonished and distressed, and he genuinely thought that she was wrong, not perhaps about the ballet but to oppose Madame. Lion went with the stream; he believed there was a tide in the affairs of men, and if he saw it, he promptly took it. People like Madame and Hilda stood against it like rocks and he regretted the waves and collisions that resulted. It had not occurred to him that it is the rocks that change the current of the stream.

Hilda had done what he would not have done, what he could not have done perhaps; that did not attract him—it, rather, shocked him—but more and more Hilda herself attracted him. She drew him like a little magnet. His future appeared to be bound up with Caroline, and up to now he had made no objection; he liked Caroline, he depended on her, in a way he had come to love her, but the tawny-haired Hilda with the lidded eyes acted on him in a strange heady and exhilarating way. It was not only Hilda herself; it was Hilda's dancing. There was a quality in it that was not in Caroline's, that he did not think was in his own. He could imagine Caroline off the stage, out of ballet, in a home, married, with children, teaching or writing poetry or keeping a hat shop; Caroline, but not Hilda. Dancing was a necessity to Hilda. The dancer in Lion recognized that and saluted it, and was drawn to her all the more. He did not want this, he even tried not to encourage it, but if she had been poison it would have been the same.

He had fallen into the habit of staying behind when he came to the school and talking over Hilda's ballets with her. At first he had not been particularly interested in the ballets; then, as Hilda talked to him about them and explained them and they danced excerpts, he had become interested. Hilda was dazzled by Lion's notice. She knew nothing of Lion's feelings for her nor of hers for him. As Mr. Felix said, "She doesn't know what she knows." Then, one evening, in the last week, she had unfolded to him her latest secret, a ballet for two dancers, based on the loud uncanny music she had shown Mr. Felix. It had excited Hilda more than any work she had done, and as she read the notes to Lion she was breathless and flushed; flushed for Hilda, which is to say she had colour below her cheekbones and her eyes were wide open . . . as if, thought Lion, trying to attend, her lids had rolled back and left her eyes unaware. . . . Lion suddenly realized he was in danger; eyes, voice, music, the whole idea of the new ballet, were sweeping him away. "Let's try it," said Hilda, but Lion knew that, then, he did not trust himself to dance with her. He was so overcome that he was rude and abrupt. He stopped the gramophone and put down the book. "I'm going now," he said.

It was like a slap in the face to Hilda. She blanched, and he saw her eyes for a moment before the lids came down; they were so mute with hurt that they had lost all power of expression. Lion's heart turned over in a strange way. He saw that he had made things worse. Till then, Hilda had not been conscious of him, as himself, but now she knew by her own hurt how much she cared. Lion tried to defend his panic. "I'm a busy person you know, my dear. I can't be always on call."

Hilda had not forgotten nor forgiven that. She had meant to be quite implacable to Lion after it, but when he had come to her, in her stress in Madame's office, his nearness and the warmth of his presence and the way he had come in for her, even if it were in the end against her, had touched her in spite of herself; she had been proof against him; she had walked past him and taken her own way. She liked to think of that, but now, in the classroom, she was intensely aware of him in the room behind her as she stood by the window.

"Hilda."

No one, and no one ever again, made her name sound as it did when Lion said it.

"Hilda."

Lion came up to the window behind her and took her elbows into his hands as he pressed them against her sides. Her elbows were warm, rounded, but in their softness he could feel the small hard strong bones.

"What strong bones you have," he said.

"I haven't," said Hilda with a sob in her breath.

"Hilda, dear!"

He heard her catch her breath again and felt the tumult of misery sweep up in her. Emotion is catching and Lion began to be in a tumult too. He pressed her closer, back against him. "Your hair smells of . . . what are those flowers that grow on bushes in London gardens? Syringa."

"London syringa smells of soot," said Hilda with a laugh that was a sob.

"Don't cry, my dear. Madame . . ."

"Madame is too great," said Hilda and her voice burnt with resentment. "She has forgotten how one begins. That one *must* begin."

Lion said nothing. He rested his cheek against her hair. It was not like Caroline's hair that was heavy, like silk; it was not as beautiful hair; it was feathery, almost like a child's, and it brushed his cheek and his eyes very lightly. For no reason he found that he was trembling and he drew back quickly. "Hilda," he began reasonably, "couldn't you . . . ?"

She turned and faced him. For her he had always been Lion, dazzling, overpowering, but since the day he had snubbed her and left her she had known he was human, like herself, like anyone . . . less than some people, thought Hilda. She had grown up; she felt old and serious and tired, because to grow much in a short while is very tiring. She saw Lion, his height and his strong shoulders, the pleasing line of his cheek. She saw the foreign olive glow of his skin, and his dark shorn curly hair. She saw all these things objectively, and for the first time she looked at his eyes. His eyes were like an Indian's, a red Indian's, quick and melting and naïve but cold. . . . I am utterly removed from him, she said proudly, but she was not. His arm came round her with urgency and he held her and said, "Hilda, give in. If you wanted to . . ."

"Do you think I don't want to?" she cried, and gave another, more heart-broken sob.

Before he could answer the others came in.

The news had spread like wildfire through the company. Now, Francis, who was War, May, the scholarship girl from Cardiff, who took Sorrow, the little Italian, Lippi, with the extraordinary *élévation*, who had been inappropriately chosen for John Smith, and Alma, and the Teacher from "Evocation," had come in. Love, Jessica Anderson, had been kept by Madame for a sharp scolding on her make-up. Alma, who was not in the first ballet, the Spanish *Cat Among the Pigeons*, wore her dress as Peace. Hilda looked at it mournfully.

"Why should Peace always be in grey?" she had asked. "In peace there is time to see colours. She should have all the colours there are."

"Then she will look like Joseph," said Madame, but the dress, designed by Mathilde Pascal from Hilda's idea, was beautiful in blue and green and violet with narrow floating petunia ribbons.

The dancers gathered round Hilda, talking, pleading,

criticizing, arguing, and quarrelling. The voices beat on her ears. She could only stand in the middle of them and say, "I am sorry."

"Madame could force you, you know," said Lippi with ferocity. He was cruelly disappointed.

"She couldn't."

"She could. She could make you pay for the dresses and the cost," said Lippi spitefully. He was feeling spiteful. It was his first big part.

"We worked on it so hard," said the Teacher. "I think you should have a little consideration for us, Hilda."

"You don't think of us at all."

"I think she is quite right," said Francis. "Madame should give all of it or none."

"You only say that because you were cut. It's better this way, Hilda. Really it is."

"Yes, really Hilda. None of us liked 'War.' "

"You are jealous, Michael, because it made 'Evocation' look weak."

" 'Evocation' couldn't look weak. It's the best thing in the ballet. Madame said so."

"Hilda. Darling. Don't, don't, don't let it be cut."

"Everyone said my 'Prologue' make a sensation, and now no sensation!" cried poor Lippi.

"Hilda, *please!*"

"Please, Hilda."

"Please, Hilda."

"No," said Hilda tight-lipped.

"But why?"

"*Why,* Hilda?"

"Why?"

"Tell them why," said Lion treacherously.

Because . . . If I had given in I should have hated myself. Now you hate me, but I can bear that, Hilda might have flung at them and him, but she said nothing, and stood there among them, tears stinging in her eyes and throat.

"Won't you change your mind?"

"Change your mind, Hilda."

"Hilda, dear."

Then Lion put his arm round her shoulders and pressed her to him and said, "Stop bullying her. She can't do what she thinks wrong. Leave her alone. She shall do exactly what she likes."

Hilda, whose face had been as white and hard as if it were carved in stone, flushed again. Her lips and her eyes and her voice quivered as she called out, "Very well. Have it. Have it as *Meditations* or as anything else that you like."

Lippi and the Teacher wrung her hands, Alma kissed her. Francis and May looked at her as if she were a traitor. But they would have been on the other side if their dances had been chosen, thought Hilda wearily. Everyone has their price. Well, mine isn't very high. The stinging in her eyes and throat grew sharper and she burst into tears.

She was aware that Lion had sent the others away with a jerk of his head. She was intensely aware that his arm was round her and that she hated his arm.

"You have done a wise thing, Hilda," said Lion and he laid his cheek against her hair. He knew it was dangerous, but he wanted to feel that light brushing again. He felt it and his lips travelled over her hair to her cheek and Hilda was filled with such despair that her tears almost choked her. She jerked her cheek away and turned back to the window.

Sounds, voices, music, the sharp clapping of a pair of hands, reached them through the open garden door of the theatre. The rehearsal had begun. They should both have been there but they did not move. It was beginning to be twilight in the garden; shut in by houses, it had an early dusk. It was twilight in the classroom too, dark on the floor, darker in the corners, dark, broken by light, in the reflections in the mirrors; they reflected Hilda and Lion and glimpses of Hilda and Lion: their hands and faces made moving patches against their dark practice clothes, and the long line of Hilda's legs and feet showed in her pink tights.

"You can't go in to rehearsal like that," said Lion. "Listen, they are playing the *pas de deux,* Liuba's first dance with John. It's such a calm little dance that it will calm you. Come and dance it with me."

"Dance it with me." He could not, at that moment, have said anything better to Hilda. She answered, "No," but, "Come," said Lion, and took her hand and led her into the middle of the floor, and, in the twilight, to the music coming from the theatre, they danced.

Lion would have said before that Hilda was not tall enough for him; now she filled what he could only feel was a womanly place beside him; she seemed exactly the right height. She danced with him, and he took her strong responsive little body in his hands, and could feel her taut against him; he could feel her muscles harden and change under his hand as he held her and supported her and held her against him, swung her, lifted her, and put her down, and held her again, below him, her back arched so that he looked down on the swelling of her breast, her throat, and her face bent back to look up at him. He saw, with a tinge of amusement, what he had not noticed before, that though her nose and brows and chin were all severely straight, her eyes were tilted . . . She is not such a little nun, thought Lion, and then he was not amused. Hilda's eyes had been closed with tears, but now, as they looked backwards up at him, they were wide open and warm and bright. Lion held her more tightly still.

Hilda was shaken out of herself by emotion. She had been angry with Lion because she was disappointed in him; then why was she so helpless and pliant that she let Lion do with her as he wished? She did not know. She had not seen this Hilda in herself before. To dance with Lion was to forget him, all except the fact that he was Lion, the superb young man. The dance between the Eldest Pupil and Interloper was tender as well as calm. "I have never known you dance like this, Hilda," said Lion.

"Haven't you?" said Hilda demurely. They were both

breathing a little faster than usual. Then he loosed her and said, "This is a boy's dance. It's too young for me. Hilda, what was that ballet you started to show me last week?"

Hilda flushed.

"You hadn't time to see it," she said crisply.

"Yes. I know, but . . . You wouldn't understand. I remember it. Let's try it now."

Hilda went to the gramophone and took two records off the shelf. She had no need to look for them. They had been there for months. She put the first of them on the turntable and switched on the gramophone, and released the catch and set the needle. The music swelled out into the room. It began gently. "That is my *adage*," said Hilda. Then it rose. It was not polite music, it was raucous and savage sweeping through the room.

"Yes, that is the one I mean," said Lion.

"Watch," said Hilda. "This is your part." She had begun on the rush of music, where it grew louder. Lion watched. They switched back the gramophone and he went through it again, Hilda beside him. Then they started again, Hilda in the solo *adage* with which the ballet opened. Though she should have been unconscious of him, Hilda was very conscious, but when the opening theme ended and he came, in the savage overbearing rush that she had worked out but never seen, she shrank back in real fear and surprise and cried out, "Lion. No!"

"Why? Why, what is the matter?" Lion was angry at

being stopped, angrier than he knew. "Why did you stop me? Isn't that right?"

"Yes . . . only . . ."

"Isn't that what you meant?" said Lion, more angry.

"Yes, but . . ."

"But what? What?"

"It's too . . . strong," said Hilda faintly.

"It can't be," said Lion. "It has to be strong. Begin again," he ordered.

She began and this time, though again she had the giddy feeling of being violently overthrown, borne backwards and mastered, she danced with him. "I don't envy her. I shouldn't like to dance that," said Alma later, watching her. "Nor should I," said Rayevskaya, and a great many of the girls in the company agreed with her. "It's too queer," said Alma, and Liuba Rayevskaya, her eyes solemn and round, said what they many of them felt, "I think it's shocking." As Hilda danced, more and more her power came up to match Lion until she was dancing so much with him that she was almost . . . within him, thought Hilda. It's only a dance, she thought giddily. It's only a dance. . . . Her hands clung, she felt his thigh lift her, force her, his breath came on her cheek and his head bent over hers. She gave a little gasp. His eyes were shut.

"And *what* is the meaning of this *deafening noise?*" asked Madame's voice in the doorway.

Chapter Three

THE rehearsal was not going well.

Madame had not come to it in a good mood. The cause of her mood, she thought, was Hilda, but was it Hilda's behaviour to her, or hers to Hilda? Madame covered that question quickly in her mind. It was Hilda.

"Isn't it sufficient, ab-so-lute-ly sufficient, that she should have been allowed to prroduce her little ballet on an occasion like tomorrow without dictating to me? A double anniversary! The reopening of the theatre and my jubilee, only I don't wish to say jubilee, it sounds like the kitchen, not? But, fifty years! Fifty years and a girl of seventeen thinks she can dictate, I ask you?" She said this to Rebecca and Miss Parkes, who neither of them, in any case, would have dared to contradict her.

Madame knew it did not matter if Hilda were young or old, old as the hills. Olways those hills, said Madame. She was also beginning to understand what Mr. Felix meant when he called Hilda an Egyptian. They are old too, thought Madame. An uncomfortable people, stiff and angular, refusing to crumble into dust like others, having themselves preserved for ever, building uncomfortable monumental sharp-edged things like pyramids and having themselves drawn with a one-eyed profile. Yes, single-eyed, said Madame, and for a moment she was arrested. If we could oll be that, and she sighed, but a moment later she said, irritated, I don't like Egyptians. Hilda will have to grow out of it, of being so marked. A dancer should have no country.

The moon is my country. Who had said that? She was beginning to be tired, or she would not have such thoughts. I am inconsequential, not? but not as bad as that. *The moon is my country.* Who said it? No one, said Madame, but she knew it was Pierrot. . . . Well, Pierrot is the no one in us oll, olways yearning. "But I don't want the moon," said Madame aloud. "I want the earth and I get what I want because I don't expect something for nothing. I expect something for something," said Madame severely. "Hilda must learn that too."

Miss Parkes and Rebecca, who had looked up in surprise, politely concurred.

Something else was running in her head. It was a sentence and nothing to do with Hilda or the performance, an echo coming from far away. Why should she hear it now? It was a small sentence, utterly detached from anything around her, with no bearing or significance that she could see. It floated detached into her head and said itself over and over again: *Listen, Niura, that is a nightingale.* No one has called me Niura for years, thought Madame. Niura. Anechka. *Listen, Niura, that is a nightingale.* She began to be annoyed. "How stupid," she said aloud. "Stupid! Silly! Obstinate!"

Rebecca and Miss Parkes searched the stage to find who was the unlucky person she was speaking of.

On the stage *Cat Among the Pigeons* had begun. Its music came in a warm sparkling torrent, with the infectious clicking rhythm of castanets, to Madame where she stood in the aisle between the stalls. The Convent Pupils in their white skirts fringed with black were circling, stamping their heels between tubs of orange trees in blossom. "Gently! Crrisply!" called Madame. "You sound like horses in a forge. Carrt horses!" said Madame.

The company knew Madame's mood to a hair. Madame was in a temper.

Not temper, temperrament, she would have said, but to the young dancers on the stage, to every man in the orchestra, to Mr. Felix conducting, to the experienced Rebecca, and to Miss Parkes standing by, it was temper, plain spoiled temper.

It affected them differently. Mr. Felix's conducting became more spontaneous as if he suddenly found it more interesting; his gloved hands moved more lightly; he always wore gloves to conduct. "They draw even more attention to your hands," said Miss Ilse. "Let them," said Mr. Felix. "They look macabre." And Madame had interfered and said, "I like them macabre." Miss Parkes felt cold, tired and helpless. She had just handed Madame the sheaf of letters with which Madame beat the rail. She had typed them that day and she could not go home until Madame had signed them . . . if there is anything left of them to sign, thought Miss Parkes hopelessly. Rebecca thought that, if she dared, she would leave. She wished she had left last Christmas or on any number of the times she had wanted to leave before that. The flautist stopped playing and thoughtfully let a trickle of saliva run out of his flute. "We shall have trouble, I think," he said to the oboe. Of the dancers on the stage, some grew resentful and looked sulky, some became stupid from fright, some danced as though the stage boards were coals and burnt their feet, and some, with stronger nerves, became excited.

In her irritability small things, almost irrelevant things, caught Madame's attention. And that is what should *not* be happening, now, thought Madame. Now I should be seeing it *whole!* This was the time for sight and strength. This is when I should pull it oll together! Have it in my hand! It is now, or never! It looked as if it would be never.

The gay insouciant *Cat Among the Pigeons* was the best of Jan Holbein's ballets. Madame had chosen it for this anniversary because of that and, as she had told the company, because sixty years ago she herself had danced, as a small child, the part that Archie was to take tomorrow, the Humming-Bird.

"A *boy* for the Humming-Bird?" asked Miss Ilse. She said it as if it would be sacrilege.

"He will be perrfect," said Madame. He was. With his extreme lightness and quickness and polish, his crest of hair, and brilliant feathered surcoat, Archie made an impression, all the more because he was a boy. Madame felt she could not have borne it had he been another girl. Every movement, every dart and line of those dances, was in her still.

There was a description of a humming-bird that Jan had read to her from a book he had had as a child . . . *the feathers on its wings and tail were black, those on its body and under its wings were of a greenish brown with a fine red cast or gloss which neither silk nor velvet could imitate. It had a small crest on its head, green at the bottom and gilded at the top, which sparkled in the sun like a little star in the middle of its forehead. Its black eyes appeared like two shining points and its bill was black and slender and about the length of a small pin. Its eggs are about the size of a small pea and white as snow and its nest is not larger than half an apricot and of the same shape and lined with cotton.* Madame read it to Archie. Archie was interested but not bewitched.

The Humming-Bird danced against the green of the Spanish-styled Brazilian garden, the black and white of the nuns, the white and black of the Convent Pupils; the music had the sound of bells dropping from the square bell-tower and was warm like the lax, sun-baked little town beyond the walls, broken by the quivering passage of the Humming-Bird. Now, though it should have had all its old enchanting quality, it was not the same. To Madame it seemed that the music dragged, that the bells were flat, the pupils lumpy; she noted that one of them, Gaby, was not wearing the required coral cross, and that John, leaping from the wall, landed with a thud that would have made any portress turn round, but these were little things. Madame's eager and powerful eye saw them all, but never, at this stage, would she do more than note them and speak about them afterwards; now she found herself wanting to stop the rehearsal. It was ostensibly for them, she did not know where the real trouble lay. She could not see it. She could not see it whole.

"No! No! No!" cried Madame, beating the orchestra rail with Miss Parkes' letters. "No! I will not have it like this. John, you are dancing like a mastodon . . . a lorry-load of bricks. Liuba, you were late on that entrance. Late! Felix! You are taking it too slow. Your tempo is oll wrong."

Mr. Felix said courteously that the tempo was the same as yesterday. "Then yesterday it was too slow. Now start again." She looked along the line of Convent Pupils and said, "You are not oll here. Who isn't here?" Several voices replied that it was Hilda.

"So! She thinks she can disobey me as well as . . . as *flout* me," said Madame, and she turned to speak to someone at her side. There was no one there. She looked into the wings. Then, "Where is Lion?" she asked.

After a pause, a voice said that he was not there. There was a longer pause.

Lion had always been by Madame when she needed him as far as it had been compatible with his own ends; they both knew it was as far as was compatible; Madame would not have had it otherwise; it was necessary for Lion to go away, to the Continent, to America, on tour. It was necessary that he should be a great deal at the Metropolitan and with his own wide circle of useful friends, but tonight there was no excuse; he should have been there when she needed him and what, who, on her ground, could be more compatible with Lion than she? A storm of anger began to come up in Madame. If she could have recognized it, she would have seen that it was the same brand of feeling that had made her choose a boy instead of a girl for the Humming-Bird, but this was stronger.

"Go strraight on! Gaby, go into Hilda's place," she said. Her eyes had a dark glitter and her hand, holding the letters, had crumpled them up. "Oh, don't do that!" Miss Parkes could have cried. "I typed them all so carefully," but Madame was oblivious of Miss Parkes. Then her voice shrilled above the orchestra.

"Liuba! You were late on your beat again. Late!"

The gay small-limbed Liuba Rayevskaya stopped almost in mid-air, turned pale and then red, her eyes bright with fear and dismay.

"Liuba Ivanovna Rayevskaya, have you no earrs?" asked Madame in a deadly small voice across the silenced orchestra. "Can—you—not—hear? I ask you those four little tiny little words. Can—you—not—hear? Ah God!" cried Madame. "Why do I have to waste my time with dolts?"

No one answered her. Mr. Felix began Rayevskaya's introduction again. She went back to her place. She was late again. Mr. Felix stopped the orchestra himself. The dancers held their breath. Rayevskaya burst into tears. Madame threw down her letters and walked out of the theatre.

Outside the theatre door she leant against the wall and closed her eyes. She felt dizzy and sick. "Ah no!" she whispered. "This isn't what I came to do. This is . . . fiasco." Madame Holbein did not have fiascos. Well? "Yes, I know," whispered Madame. "It is in my hands." Her hands were not light and gloved like Mr. Felix's, they were firm and experienced, but sometimes they were too hard. Not many days ago she had caught Archie pinching a little girl in class; Archie liked to pinch the little girls on their chests and small plump hams. "Now I shall pinch you, Archie," Madame had said, "and my fingers are harrd, harrd from playing castanets." Hard from castanets perhaps, but also from pulling, jerking, tweaking, tugging, smoothing, moulding. Experienced hands can mould what is malleable almost to what they will, if they know when they have gone too far. She saw the little Rayevskaya's terrified blue eyes. "Ah! No. No!" cried Madame. "She will never dance like that. Ah no!"

To calm herself she began to walk up and down the

garden, where it was not yet dark but where the green was made dim by the lit oblongs and squares thrown on the grass and across the bushes by the lighted windows of the theatre. It was cool in the garden after the crowd and heat inside; its coolness fell on her face and neck and hands, but to her it was cold and she huddled her shoulders in her jacket. "Does she sleep in it?" the children sometimes said. Only Lollie could see nothing wrong in Madame's jacket. "It is the colour of pansies," said Lollie. She had seen pansies.

To teach, to direct, is to correct and criticize, to change and widen vision, to lead, but it is also to know when to leave alone . . . and when to capitulate. That is what Madame Holbein found hardest of all to do. Perhaps she had never quite learnt it.

Now she walked up and down the garden, down and up, trying to bring herself to it, to the moment when she must go back into the theatre and start again.

She began to think of the ballet and now, as she had wanted, she began to see it as a whole, to see what was needful and what she must do. She began to work it out, and, as she thought of it, this work that was her own and utterly familiar began to lay its own quiet and steadiness on her; with all its alarums and fireworks, it was steady and it was quiet, and it was patient. "Madame is so impatient," the pupils, everyone, said, but she was infinitely patient. It was sixty years since she had run in the feathered coat of which Archie's was the replica across that far-off stage in Buenos Aires; fifty since she had made her debut as a finished dancer . . . but a dancer is never finished, never . . . and it seemed to Madame now, truthfully, that she had not rested for a day since . . . because even when I was resting I was planning.

Tomorrow Archie would dart, every nerve alive in a tumultuous effort to please, his eyes hot and dry, his cheeks burning, his heart beating like a clapper with excitement. It happened again, in every season, with every performance, with each entrance of each dance. Time passes, that is what they say, but that is what it doesn't do, said Madame. In each one, with each one, Madame lived through it again. It left her exhausted, but that was why she lived.

"How do you do all you do?" they asked her. "How could I not do it?" she might have answered. She was in Archie, as she was in Rayevskaya and John and Lion and Caroline and Bianca and Michel and Lointaine, all the names, down to the little ones, down to the new little Miette, that crumb of a child. Now, this moment, she was Rayevskaya, whom she had frightened out of her sturdy native wits; she was John who stood beside Rayevskaya, and every dancer in the ballet, Archie, Jessica, Michael, May, Gaby, Hilda . . . Hilda! No, she could not bring herself to be Hilda.

All at once Madame became aware that, while the theatre was muted, waiting, music was streaming from the house, where all but the dressing-room windows were dark. It was blatant loud music of a curious impoliteness.

She stood for a moment, listening, startled. Where is Ilse? she thought. She should have been in the office, but the office was dark. She has gone over to see the nuns, thought Madame furiously. She is never here when I want her, never! Madame could still move quickly; she went through the dressing-rooms and up the back staircase like a whirlwind and threw open the classroom door. "And *what* is the meaning of this *deafening noise?*" asked Madame's voice on the threshold.

Madame did not know what it was that Hilda and Lion were dancing; she saw only that they were dancing together, that Lion was dancing with Hilda while she, Madame, was left to take the rehearsal alone. The whole of her changed to spite. How dare you! she could have cried to Hilda. Let me tell you that oll this, this, is nothing at oll that you think. He is Lion. Lion . . . and you are a crude little girl; crrude and arrogant and conceited and vain and sly. No, he is not for you. Hold your tongue. Don't speak to me, cried Madame as Hilda raised her head, but neither of them had said a word.

Hilda had been standing with her back to the door so that the shock of Madame's voice had been greater. Lion had seen her and stayed his rush. He did not look very disconcerted. He took a long leap towards Madame and finished in front of her. "I have been talking to Hilda. She has come round," he said triumphantly. "Now we can all agree."

For a moment, Madame was more angry than ever. She felt cheated. I can't even be angry in peace, she thought for the second time that evening. Lion had brought her up too sharply. She felt angry with Lion too. He shows his teeth too much when he smiles, she thought. You wouldn't notice that of course, you little fool, she flung silently at Hilda. He has bewitched you . . . but she knew that, if there had been any bewitching, it was Hilda who had bewitched Lion, and she herself had not noticed his teeth before.

"You are pleased?" said Lion. "Say you are pleased."

She had to be pleased, though she still hardly knew how she had come to be in this position. Hilda, she felt, had turned the tables on her. "I am pleased, if it's trrue," she said grudgingly, and glared at Hilda.

Hilda was angry too. Madame, in the doorway, had given her a shock and a nasty little premonition of knowledge that she would rather have been without. She was angry against Madame, angrier with Lion, and most angry with herself.

"Is this true, Hilda?"

"Yes, Madame," said Hilda, and closed her lips; but she knew she had closed them too late. She felt she was a Judas.

"It is very sudden, not?" said Madame looking at her and keeping her eyes away from Lion.

"Yes, Madame."

"You are quite sure?"

"Yes, Madame."

"Then, if you have finished . . . being talked round," said Madame dryly, "we had better go to the theatre."

As they came into the theatre they were greeted by

stricken silence. All the heads came round towards them, Madame could even see Archie's crest under John's arm. Did they think I should never come back? thought Madame. I wonder what they would have done, not? It did not occur to her that they might have gone home, nor to them. Her amusement left her as she saw Rayevskaya's round face nearly haggard with unhappiness. The dancers were grouped ready for a new entrance, the portress was in her place, the two nuns in the garden; Mr. Felix, holding his baton, smoothed a wrinkle from the back of his left glove with his one good right-hand finger; Miss Parkes was flattening the mutilated letters on her knee; Rebecca had evidently been parleying with all of them, she looked hot and tired, but now no word was spoken, no one moved.

Madame came down from the garden door to the orchestra rail. "Liuba," she called. "Liubochka, come here."

John pushed the shrinking Rayevskaya forward.

"Now, dearr child!" said Madame, "I want you to go back from the dance of the two pupils. Hilda, go and dress and take your place. Now, Liubochka, dearr child, from where you brreak away towards John: *attitude . . . pirouettes . . . entrechat volée . . .* You remember? So! Yes. Lion, I want you to watch this *particularly*. I have never seen you, Liubochka, do as well before. Now! Do you see, Lion?" Rayevskaya, encouraged, let herself dance. "You see, Lion. Give it a moment longer, Liuba, a little more weight, a little more of the head. So! Ex-cel-lent! Go on from there." Rayevskaya, surprised and dazzled, went on,

Madame nodded to Mr. Felix, the others slipped into their places, and the rehearsal began again.

Soon Madame saw it was gathering the impetus it needed; it grew smooth and clear. She was sure that Mr. Felix had quickened his pace. Rayevskaya was heartened and relieved by the praise just as Madame had meant her to be, and began to dance with the grace of a little swallow. How artless they are, thought Madame, and sighed. It was almost boring; then she caught sight of Hilda, come back in her fringed skirts to whirl among the others. Not oll of them, thought Madame. Her smile changed to a frown as she looked at Lion watching in the wings. Exactly as she had guessed, he was watching Hilda. "Tchk-tchk!" said Madame, and turned her attention to the rehearsal. I have other things to think of than about the two of them.

She did not think about them, but she had to think persistently of Hilda's ballet. She had a strong impulse, now that she had won her point, to leave it alone. Leave it altogether or cut it, said Madame's instinct. That means cut it, said her brain. And you have nothing to put in its place. *Cat Among the Pigeons, The Noble Life,* that isn't an adequate programme. Then you must keep it and be expedient, said her brain.

That was that word again, the word she had said she would not consent to use. It tasted no better than it had before. But words do *not* have tastes, thought Madame sharply. She did not know what to do, and again she had a quite unpredicted instinct to do nothing at all. "But I can't, *now!* At the eleventh minute," cried Madame. "I can't do nothing."

"What is there to do now?" asked Lion who had come down to join her. "Isn't it all settled?"

Madame did not answer. She knew that it was not.

With final quietness in its music *Cat Among the Pigeons* was drawing to its end. The last flick of the heels of the Interloper was gone, the last of his friends had gone back over the wall where he belonged; the Nun read aloud, the Pupils were grouped round her with their round frames and long white pieces of embroidery; the sound of bells fell into the garden, the gate was shut; the Humming-Bird made its last quick flight and each Pupil lifted her head and stole a glance at the next, the Nun continued to read aloud, and the curtain came down.

It immediately went up again for Madame to say what she thought to the company. The dancers waited tensely; each one of them knew, or thought he or she knew, what he or she had done or not done, but Madame said nothing. She looked at them as if she did not see them and then roused herself to say, "That will do. Now go and change, oll of you," and to Rayevskaya, "Bravo!" Then she called Hilda and told her to fetch the dancers who had roles in *Lyre*. They came down off the stage and stood round while Madame explained the new dance order to them.

"Each separate. No attempt to link them. Yes, Hilda?"

"Yes, Madame."

Madame felt Mr. Felix looking at her. She looked back

at him. Who said Felix's eyes are like forget-me-nots? she thought irritably. They are. They say *forget me not* as if he were reminding . . . She turned her back on him. Mr. Felix came round and spoke to her. "What about the harpist?" he said. "You won't want him now. He played only for John Smith in the 'Prologue' and 'Epilogue,' and now you have no lyre."

"No. No lyre," said Madame.

"Pity. He was a guinea a rehearsal and he has done six," said Mr. Felix.

Hilda followed him back to the orchestra and stood there beside the rail.

"Mr. Felix . . ."

"You are an appeaser," said Mr. Felix severely.

"It . . . it is of no use standing up to Madame."

"It is of use," said Mr. Felix, making a huge cross from margin to margin across the page with his blue pencil. "One day we shall get to the end of this music *mince*," said Mr. Felix.

Madame made Hilda try the *Meditations* through, standing at her side. They did not speak to one another, nor to Lion who, as Hilda's co-producer, stood beside them too. When it was finished, there was complete silence.

"Well, what do you think of it?" asked Madame. "Well, is it better or isn't it? Haven't you a tongue? Can't you say?"

Hilda could not say because she did not know. She had only one feeling about it and that was the same she had had in the office that they had called unreasonable: It isn't my ballet. She said it aloud, "It isn't my ballet." She spoke quite unlike Hilda, she spoke stupidly, but Madame again knew that she was right. Before, it had at least been a ballet, now it was not anything; it was meaningless. Hilda looked at Madame. Do *you* like it? her look said. It had been on the tip of Madame's tongue to say, "Very well, put it oll back. At least it was interesting before," but, when she caught that look, she read it as a taunt and her resentment against Hilda flared up again. Before she knew what she had done, she had called the dancers off the stage. "It won't do," said Madame. "I can't have it."

"Then . . . what . . ." began Lion.

"I don't know," said Madame, "but not this. Not this."

"Let me call them tomorrow at ten," said Lion. "We can work on it . . ."

"No."

"Then?"

"I don't know."

"But . . . You must decide. If not now, tomorrow. There *is* only tomorrow," said Lion, and he paused. "There *isn't* tomorrow," he said. "Tomorrow is the day."

But that instinct, more powerful now, told Madame that she must not decide, that she should leave it alone. "No, leave it alone," she said aloud.

"But . . . Madame . . ." Lion looked at her as if she were mad.

"Ah, Lion! Don't conflict me so. I beg you. I am getting

tired out. We shall go strraight on to *Noble Life*. Hilda, why are you standing there? Go and change. Everrybody go and change. Are we oll to wait for you, not?"

The Noble Life had been arranged as a ballet for Madame at the height of her career. It had been her own idea, taken from the tapestries in the Cluny Museum. She had been helped in the choreography by her old teacher, Bellini, and the music had been arranged for it from chorales and songs of sixteenth-century French music. Even Mr. Felix approved of the music. The sets and dresses had been taken from the tapestries. They had been kept with the same thought and care with which she had kept all her wardrobe. "It is perrfectly possible to conserrve everrything, if you are careful enough," said Madame. She did not pause to think how she would have conserved them without Miss Ilse and Zanny. "Set, dresses, music, choreography, are parts of a single vision, of the whole idea," she said. "They should *not* be changed." Now the clothes had been copied, where necessary, or their originals worn; the sets were faded, but Madame's friend, the disreputable Noel Streete, had repainted them. "He has kept them ex-act-ly the same," said Madame. "They tell me Noel is olways drrunk and gone to pieces, but I tell you he can still paint and he has rrespect," said Madame, "and that is more than some ones have." The sets were from the background of the tapestries, fleurettes on a dark-blue ground.

Madame's dress as the Lady was too small for Caroline. That was disappointing. She had given one of her own

parts to Archie, but this was far more personal. She felt
that it was only to Caroline that she could have given this,
relinquished it, because no one but herself had ever danced
the Lady. "There were two or three changes for the Nobleman," she told Caroline, "but the Lady was entirely mine,
mine. It was the last part I ever danced." Now, the dress
would not fit. "But I was wrrong for the Lady," said Madame generously. "She should have been fair and tall as
Caroline is, and I was not." Still, she was disappointed.

Why do I mind about this ballet? she asked herself. Was
I perhaps a little in love with my partner? But she could
not remember who those partners were, and there had been
two or three of them as the Nobleman. No, I wasn't in
love . . . not with my parrtner, said Madame. Was I ever
in love? I suppose I was, but I can't remember it now.
Niura. That is a nightingale. It was not a nightingale she
heard but the sound of birds, sleepy, hazy, distant, in an
English garden. He sent me roses, each time I danced the
Lady, said Madame slowly, but who was he? She tried to
think but she could think only of Lion. He followed me
wherever I went . . . but not for long. One season. No
more, but I went on dancing, without him and his roses.
Madame lifted her chin. *Listen, Niura . . .* I must be
very tired, said Madame.

She turned her attention to the stage. "Tell them we
shall go strraight on, Rebecca."

"But we can't go straight on," said Rebecca. "Caroline
hasn't come."

Madame asked for Lion.

"He is telephoning, Madame."

Madame knew he was telephoning the Metropolitan. In a few minutes he came back and his face was clouded. Lion hated trouble and here was trouble. "More trouble," said the flautist to the oboe.

"She is on her way, Madame. She will be here directly."

Madame looked at him without pretence, steadily. "What was Caroline dancing at the Metropolitan tonight?"

"*Sylphides*, the 'Prelude.'"

"Only *Sylphides*?"

"Yes."

"She should have been here by now," said Madame. She asked quietly, "Who is her understudy?"

"Hilda," said Rebecca.

Madame frowned. "I should like Liuba to try it," said Madame.

"She doesn't know it, Madame."

"Then Alma."

"Alma!" Lion spoke in surprise. "But . . . you gave the understudy to Hilda."

"Did I?" said Madame. "Yes, I did. Why did I?"

"Alma isn't up to it, Madame," said Lion. "Caroline is on her way," he said diplomatically. "Better wait for her."

"No," said Madame proudly.

"Then let Hilda stand in for her until she comes." He was ready to go on in the Nobleman's silks and velvets. She

knew he wanted to dance it with Hilda and that made her
struggle all the sharper.

"Call Hilda then," she said.

Hilda came off the stage. She was in her dress as the
Waiting Maid with the Mirror in the embroidery scene.

"You will dance Caroline's part."

"Yes, Madame."

"You know it?"

"Yes, Madame."

Madame felt that Lion, beside her, was watching and
looking. She herself noticed how, once again, Hilda's eyes
were illuminated when she was pleased and she noticed, as
Lion had done, that the angle at which they were set was
provocative. You are not going to have this quite oll your
own way, she could have told Lion then, and to her surprise
that gave her a perverse feeling of pleasure. As if women
were bonded together, thought Madame, even I and Hilda.

"Gaby must go into your part," she told Hilda. "It will
be experrience for her."

Gaby's face shone equally with Hilda's. Madame was
touched by that. "How good they are! How nice it is to
please them!" she said to Lion. "They may be simple, young,
not hearrd of, but they are better to work with, Lion, than
your ballerinas. They are fresh and earrnest. I should like
to give them oll a chance with the good parrts . . . oll that
deserve it, that is." Her eye had fallen on a group waiting
on the stage. "Jessica! And what are you doing?"

"N-nothing Madame."

"Then to do nothing is to go kicking and twisting about like a bag full of bones? You will stand still, *still*, even if it is for hours while I am talking, not? You will have the manners, the rrespect to wait for me."

The curtain came down and went up on the first scene, "The Walk."

With Lion on the stage there came to Madame a complete sense of rest. Lion, as a dancer, had come into his prime; she had no need to trouble about him, she could take her reward and joy in the sureness of his power. I see you, Lion, Madame might have said. There is no need to magnify you because you are big enough. He was big, strong, and virile; he had none of the air of girlishness, the pallor, of John, or even Francis, or so many male dancers. Lion was male, with male zest and male strength. Yes, you are a lord of creation, thought Madame, watching him.

He was singularly beautiful in the Nobleman's clothes. The dark velvet doublet made his skin look darker. Dark as . . . ivy, thought Madame, or velvet itself, like Romeo, but that is wrrong. In this ballet it is the Lady who should be beautiful. She had a pang of sheer jealousy when she thought of Hilda in her place as the Lady. Hilda won't hold a candle to him, she thought with jealous satisfaction, but when Hilda came on, Madame was surprised to see how well she looked and how she matched Lion. "She has her own beauty, a quality of beauty," Madame was surprised into saying to Rebecca.

"I have always thought so," Rebecca answered.

"She isn't tall enough," said Madame quickly, and surprised herself still more by adding, "Neither was I. But no one noticed it," she chuckled. "I had such dignity."

"So has Hilda," said Rebecca, and, for once, she was unconscious of Madame's frown.

It was true. Though Hilda's head was not on a level with Lion's cheek, she had a dignity that made her tall. "Head and shoulders out of his reach," said Madame, "and that is how she should be."

For a moment the figures of Lion and Hilda swam uncertainly in front of her eyes. She was on the stage, under the lights, the pearls of the head-dress touched her cheek and she tossed back the ermine lappets of her sleeves and saw her hand coming small from the frilled cuff of the embroidered under-sleeve. Watching Caroline's interpretation she had forgotten her own. Now Hilda brought it startlingly to life. She . . . she . . . thought Madame, and she cried, "Who taught her this?"

"No one," said Rebecca.

"No one. The little upstart. How dare she," said Madame.

For the second time that day, Lion danced with Hilda. "Take it calmly. Don't press it," he whispered to her. "Let it happen. Don't take pains now. You can do it, easily." He did not know the half of what Hilda could do and, as he danced with her, he began to be puzzled. It was different from Caroline. As they danced, he felt Hilda draw more and more away from him and he wondered more and more why, until he saw that she was in part; he was not Lion, he was the importunate Nobleman and she the aloof Lady. That piqued him.

Lion knew, without a shadow of doubt, of his effect on Hilda. He had had adulation and flattery, sometimes even adoration. He knew that this young serious green-eyed girl loved him in spite of herself, and because he was innately gentle it touched him; he was beginning to have a tender feeling for Hilda that was quite apart from her attraction for him.

Behind them, the pages were walking with long garlands of leaves and flowers in the maze dance that linked the scenes. Now Lion had to draw Hilda on one side, his arm, the Nobleman's arm, round her. "Hilda. We dance well together, don't we?"

"Hush."

The Attendant, Francis, with the falcon on his wrist, was on in the opening of "Departure for the Hunt." In a minute Lion would have to leave her after an embrace, a stage embrace, but Hilda thought of it with quickened breath.

"Hilda . . ."

"Hush."

His arm was holding her, a stage arm it was true, but Lion's arm. She was pressed against him, his cheek was against her cheek. The stage spun round her, but it still had an axis on which it could spin and she remained cool and clear in her head.

"Hilda, you are a little iceberg."

"Hush." But then he had to turn her, hold her, with her face towards him; before she bent backwards and away from him, she smiled at him from under her lids, and it was a smile of pure happiness.

Madame clapped her hands. The orchestra stopped and there beside Madame was Caroline.

> *"Egypt's might is tumbled down,*
> *Down a-down the deeps of thought . . ."*

said Mr. Felix to Hilda in the pause while they were waiting for Caroline to dress. If Mr. Felix had ever been sufficiently interested to be cruel, Hilda thought, he was cruel then. "I was only standing in for Caroline," she said with dignity.

Caroline was gracious. She had a wait in the wings and Hilda, as her Maid, was beside her. She could have ignored Hilda, but Caroline was gracious. "You danced that part very well. Very well, did you know?" she said kindly.

"I know," said Hilda. That was a queer rude answer for a chit of a pupil to give to a dancer in Caroline's position and it was accompanied by such a blaze in those green eyes that Caroline's own, always wide open, opened wider in astonishment.

Once Caroline was on the stage it became obvious that Hilda had no real beauty at all. "Now they are in their rright places," said Madame, satisfied. They were where she would have them be, Caroline partnered with Lion. Lion drew the circle in the air . . . you are beautiful . . . in front of Caroline's face. It could not have been more true. "She has everything in that face," Madame had often said, but now, watching her, it seemed she had not . . . everything. Caroline's every movement was pure, classical . . . arristocratic, said Madame, watching her, and surely that was right for the Lady? But . . . was Caroline's Lady a little moon-faced? Did she lack spice after . . . ? Madame caught herself up, but she could not help remembering the precision and lightness of Hilda's attack.

"What do you think, Rebecca?" she said aloud.

Rebecca was watching and Madame saw she was puzzled. "Hilda has come on tremendously in this last year," said Rebecca.

I asked you what you were thinking of *Caroline*, Madame might have said, but she saw that Rebecca's thoughts matched her own.

But . . . even if Caroline is different, that ought not to matter, thought Madame. There is plenty of room for difference. It makes it more interesting, not? She began to see that the trouble lay, not in the difference, but in Caroline herself. She could not bear that. She covered it quickly. "Look at their two faces," began Madame to Rebecca. Caroline's had a pleasing gentle brow, a smooth fair skin, rounded curves of chin and mouth and nose; Hilda's was straight, severe, though she had those tip-tilted eyes. "Hilda can look ugly," said Madame. "Caroline could never by any chance look ugly."

"Hilda can look anything," said Rebecca, and smiled.

"She is a cold calculating little . . ." But Madame knew that Hilda was not. She was relentless, but she could also be reckless and generous; she would give herself away, over and over again. She gave herself away in her parts. "Overdanced them," Madame had said. Caroline never overdanced. "It is interesting that, in Hilda," said Madame, in spite of herself, "that she should be strrong, headstrong often, and yet she has real restrraint in her ballets."

"Hilda can discipline all except her feelings," said Rebecca, and she added, "That may be hard for her. She has more feeling than most."

Madame saw the difference in their eyes; Hilda's lidded into secrecy perhaps but, in moments, wide open, giving her away, transparent with vision; and Caroline's, always open, larger, finer, with heavy silk lashes, but bland, opaque —and Madame knew, and knew she had always known, that they were slightly too close together. "Caroline's grandfather was a wool merchant who made nearly a million pounds," she said suddenly to Rebecca.

But Madame loved Caroline. For few people Madame felt love; for things, very many things, but few people.

"When Caroline was my age," asked the zealous Lollie, "was she a much better dancer than me?"

"Say 'I,' Lollie."

"But was she?"

"You haven't starrted yet," said Madame. "And you will never starrt if you don't worrk at that *battement, battement-*

en-ronde, Lollie. In waves, Lollie; that does not mean to zigzag up and down. Contrrol your foot. Contrrol it. Caroline? Caroline came to me from the very beginning. She had no faults like these, that I can*not* bear, to erradicate."

"And was she *so* good? So very, very good?"

"Ah!" said Madame with a far-away warm look. "There has only been one Caroline."

Now she was seeing flaws. She watched more closely. Caroline had been away on tour with the Metropolitan Company in Holland. One of the leading dancers had been ill and stayed behind and Caroline had been given some of her roles. She had had a small ovation and notice in the press, and when they came back to London she found herself promoted to them. She had been pleased—"Naturrally," said Madame—and better pleased with herself. Now she had come from her larger world to this small outworn one, and an old monotonous family world . . . and she thinks this will pass, thought Madame and she hunched herself in her jacket and watched with gimlet eyes.

In the Holbein Company all members took their turn in the corps de ballet; Rayevskaya, Hilda, John, Francis, and Alma were its principals, but they were subject to that discipline no less than the others. Lion, producing under Madame, obeyed her, but Caroline had position and dignity, was a guest artiste, dancing for Madame by courtesy of the Metropolitan Company, as indeed was Lion; Caroline was now in no way Madame's pupil; as a member of the Metropolitan Company she was taught by their ballet master. Madame's hands were tied. Worse, her tongue was tied. She could do nothing but stand and watch the girl in whom she had so much belief. What has happened to her? thought Madame. The answer began to be plain. Caroline was not trying. "So," Madame whispered, "she doesn't think it worrth her while to try for me."

Miss Ilse had come in and stood beside her. "This is a terrible evening," she said to Miss Ilse.

"Anna. You want your supper."

"Supper! How can I think about supper?" She put out her hand to Miss Ilse.

"How cold you are! At least let me fetch you a hot drink." Madame shook her head.

"Some *vin sucré*, hot, Anna."

"No. Don't go. I want you." She wanted Miss Ilse, who was accustomed, intimate. "Is this rehearsal never going to end?" she said.

"You must have nearly finished, Anna."

Madame shook her head, again.

She could not let it end. At the close, when the curtain had come down, gone up, she had to say, "Again. Oll over again."

The girls went back to the opening group; John and Francis, the small Lippi, and the other young men, to the wings right and left. There were murmurs which Madame allowed to go unrebuked.

"Madame . . ."

"Well, Caroline?"

"I have been dancing since this morning. Rehearsal and the performance and now this."

"What do you expect if you take part in two companies?" asked Madame. "Do you think I shouldn't rehearse you, not?"

"Madame . . ." began Lion.

"There is nothing to say, Lion," said Madame.

Caroline's gaze flickered and fell. Mr. Felix polished his baton thoughtfully with his glove.

"What about the orchestra?" asked Lion.

"What about it?" asked Mr. Felix.

"Will you stay?"

"Like you, we will stay as long as it's necessary," said Mr. Felix. It sounded like a snub.

Everyone was tired. There had been an atmosphere of strain and discord in the theatre all evening. It was not only that Madame was cross; they were used to that and, in some ways, they appreciated it because it stimulated them and made them brace themselves for an extra effort, but they knew that something was wrong. "Fundamentally wrong," said John to Hilda, who shrugged her shoulder at him crossly too.

"What do you think will happen?" asked John, as everyone was asking.

"I don't know," said Hilda.

"What do you think she will do?"

"How do I know?" said Hilda.

"Tomorrow?"

No one knew what would happen tomorrow.

Outside, in the Avenue, the theatre doors were open for booking and the bills were displayed:

HOLBEIN BALLET
Gala Anniversary Performance

Cat Among the Pigeons
(Jan Holbein)

The Noble Life
(Holbein-Bellini)

Lyre with Seven Strings
(Hilda French)

They were in the theatre ticket agencies too, in the sides of the moving staircases in the Underground stations, all over London. Would they now have to be changed, all over London? "But there wouldn't be time," said Hilda.

"They could paste those narrow papers over you," said John. "Over your name. But what will they put on them? *"Meditations?"*

"My name shouldn't go under that," said Hilda. "It's not mine."

They were all tired. The girls had unusually brilliant eyes, their make-up had run a little, their hair was untidy. The men looked sulky, their faces were sticky and pale. Caroline was cross and even Lion was put out. As he danced with Caroline he was increasingly disappointed. Nonsense, thought Lion. She is my favourite partner. It's a wonderful thing for me to have the chance to dance with her. He still felt disappointed. Mr. Felix had not spoken to his orchestra

nor they to him; Miss Parkes drooped in her stall, the val-
iant Rebecca stood beside Madame, Miss Ilse had gone.

Madame stood there, in front, her jacket wrapped round
her; she tottered a little on her feet but her eyes were still
quick, they missed nothing. The lights burnt on; if they had
been candles they would have burnt down long ago. At last
it was over. The curtain fell, went up, everyone waited, and
again Madame said nothing.

It was Lion who spoke. "Madame, some of the girls have
to catch a bus or a train home. They will miss the last if you
don't let them go now."

Madame at last opened her lips and said, "Very well."

"Do you want them tomorrow?"

"No."

"But, Madame . . ."

"No, I tell you. Not before evening." She saw consterna-
tion on his face. "I shall see tomorrow," said Madame.

Caroline came to say good night. "Madame, you look so
tired."

"I am not tirred. I don't allow myself to be tired until I
have things right." Her eyes had a look of disdain that
Hilda knew well but that Caroline had never seen before.

Caroline hesitated. Then she kissed Madame smoothly
and went away. Madame's face, as she looked after her, was
tired and very old.

All over London they will be pasting out my name. Hilda
did not know in the least if this was to be true, but she was

too tired to think coherently and John's words had lodged in her head. All over London. She saw those strips, pasted down, blotting her out . . . forever, thought Hilda dramatically. They none of them knew what was to happen, but Hilda knew in her bones that neither *Lyre with Seven Strings* nor *Meditations* would be done. Then why did she say it was good? asked Hilda bitterly. She said more bitterly, And I needn't have given in. It did no good to give in. Why did I give in?

Before, though she was equally desolate, she had had a strong feeling of pride, almost of grandeur, to sustain her in her loneliness. Now that was gone. She was like the rest of them, like anybody else. I can't even despise them now, thought Hilda. That should, of course, have been a good thing; it is not good to be conceited, but for Hilda it was strangely necessary. She was conceited, but for her it was truth.

She had come up to the classroom to put her notes and records away before anybody found them, but now she was too tired even to do that. Let them find them, said Hilda. What do I care? If I stop now I shall miss my bus. She made no effort to go and catch her bus. She stood by the window as she had stood that evening; she had fallen into the same pose but she was far more unhappy. Outside it was dark, though the theatre was still lit. I suppose Madame is still there, tearing me to pieces, thought Hilda. . . . Below the ridge, street after street, tier below tier, was lit. The lights stretched below her in uneven chains of light, from windows upstairs and windows down, but now, mostly, from windows upstairs; there were street lights and the passing lights of buses and cars and, farther away, a ball of light, a dome or bubble in the sky, the brilliant rolling West End world. That is where I thought my name would be, said Hilda, leaning her forehead on the cold glass.

Lion has gone home now, perhaps he has taken Caroline home, or he is with Madame, discussing me. Why did they say it was good? asked Hilda, a tear rolling down her nose. Madame isn't fair. She gives with one hand and takes back with the other. Why did she say it was good?

Madame had not said it was good. "Why should it be good?" said Madame. "Think what it takes to make something good. Who are you?"

That question seemed to go rolling out into the darkness among the lights.

The lights stretched in millions and, for each, there was, not a name in lights, but one little window. Like any other window, said Hilda. And each one is someone, no one. The glass was growing warm now from the pressure of her forehead, but she pressed it against it more tightly.

That is the tragedy, said Hilda, or the comedy . . . and she tried to laugh. Each someone is no one. No one, said Hilda, and the tears splashed down on the window-sill. No one; wanting, yearning, but with no power to do what they want. "Isn't it enough that you can do it at oll?" asked Madame. No, it isn't enough, cried Hilda. Not for me.

"You are very conceited." They all said that.

Yes, I am, said Hilda. I am, and I always shall be. The lights slid together in a blur of tears.

There was a rustle beside her and she looked down. The child Lollie was at her elbow.

"Lollie! You here at this time of night! You ought to have gone home hours ago."

"I can't go home," said Lollie. "Auntie can't have me alone in the flat, and Mrs. Zannger kept her."

"Your aunt is Miss Porteus?"

"Yes," said Lollie without enthusiasm.

Like Hilda, Lollie was oppressed. Like Hilda, it was partly tiredness and, like her, again, the difficulties were real. "There is a way round every difficulty," said Madame. "In dancing they don't exist." She took no excuses. She did not excuse herself.

Lollie was oppressed, but she had boundless tenacity. She had, under her fears and starts, more tenacity than anyone in the school, even Lion. Lollie would have scorned to be as anxious for her own ends as Lion. She had far more tenacity than Hilda, almost more than Madame. She had only to get over her initial fright. Where many of the young dancers gave the impression of being avid, as Madame herself was sometimes avid, Lollie gave the impression of holding back, of a naturally timed restraint that seemed to say that, with the unfolding of time, in her own time Lollie would do everything she promised and that it was her business to do. The grownups liked her. They found her restful and strong. Can a child be restful and strong? Lollie was, and this quality showed clearly in her dancing. Her torments were minor compared to her strength.

"In London today," Madame told them, "there are thousands of girls who learn dancing; in London alone, not counting Paris or New York or other great cities, nor all the towns and little towns. Of those thousands, a few hundreds perhaps think themselves as good as you do. Of those few hundreds, perhaps a hundred are ready, as dancers, for their debut to the public every year; but there are few companies, four or five or six perhaps, and, among them, they may have three, five, or shall we say, eight, places to offer to those hundred dancers."

"Eight could get in," said Lollie.

"Yes, and what happens to the other ninety-two?"

"What happens to the eight?" said Lollie.

None of this feeling communicated itself to Hilda, who stood leaning against the window and then stood back and pushed it up and leant out. The light wind blew from the theatre and brought with it a scent of flowers to the half-open window. "It doesn't smell like London, does it?" said Lollie.

Hilda paid no attention to the flowers. Could I hear talking in the theatre from here? she was wondering. The lights are still on. Is she still thinking or discussing? Or is it decided now? She felt again it was decided. Yes, my ballet is gone, thought Hilda. Gone. Still-born.

She had no inkling of feeling that she would write others; for her, tonight, it was finished. The child was dead. She was even serene in the sad calm that comes after a death. There was no more to do. It was over. The thought that she was still fertile, that there would be others, had not come to her yet, or if it came she discarded it. No, it is too difficult, Hilda might have said. It is too heart-breaking. And what good is it, to do it against the whole world? The world is too big, said Hilda. Anything I can do would make a mark no bigger than a fly's leg, if it made a mark at all. Why sweat and worry and strive and spoil all my life for this? I won't, said Hilda.

"There are thousands of girls," Madame said.

Yes, too many, thought Hilda.

"Eight places to offer to those hundred dancers," said Madame.

Ninety-two don't get in. What happens to those ninety-two? thought Hilda.

Madame . . . Madame doesn't understand, said Hilda. She is too great. Madame looked down from the past. Hilda and the other young ones were thrusting up from the present, and the present she was sure was more difficult than any Madame had known. But is it? Madame might have said, Isn't it olways the same? If it isn't one thing, it is another that makes it difficult. It must be difficult, said Madame. . . . No, said Hilda, it couldn't possibly in any time have been as difficult as it is today. We all think that, said Madame. This was the kind of maddening, monotonous dialogue Hilda often held with Madame. I wish we could cut ourselves off from the past, she said impatiently, but one

can never do that. In ballet especially, we have to do this
. . . this ancestor-worship! said Hilda. . . .

"Look at the lights," said Lollie.

"Yes," said Hilda. She did not want to look at them.

"It's hard to tell where the lights leave off and the stars
begin," said Lollie, and she said, "I have been learning the
names of the stars in school."

"I used to hate that," said Hilda. "When they used to
say we were a pin-point in the universe, I used to feel as if
the whole earth dwindled away and I was lost. It used to
frighten me."

"I don't know," said Lollie judiciously. "When they say
that, then I think, well, we are a star as well."

"Don't wait for me, Lion," said Madame. "I will put out
the lights."

Everyone else had left the theatre. Lion, waiting for
Madame in the doorway, looked broad-shouldered and
heavy and comforting. But I had better not be comforted,
thought Madame, I have work to do. "Go," she said to Lion,
but he still waited.

"It was a disastrous evening, not?"

"Not disastrous, difficult."

And this was to have been my climax, the crown, thought
Madame. She looked round the theatre and it was adept in
answering her thought. Yes, it said, you made me ready for
this. "I had planned . . ." said Madame, and broke off.

"A bad rehearsal makes a good performance."

"My *dearr* Lion!"

"Anyone can make a mistake," persisted Lion.

"When they are young, not when they are old," said Madame. "It is too late for me to make a mistake."

One mistake is not a tragedy. No, agreed Madame. But what else is it? She was tired, disappointed, worried, and grieved. Tomorrow was close. It was almost here.

"Wait till tomorrow," said Lion, and he said helplessly, "You never know."

"Tchk-tchk!" said Madame. "Go home, Lion, before you drrive me mad."

Lion went home. One by one, lingeringly, she turned out the lights. She locked the outer doors, walking across the stage, which was set again for Jan's Brazilian garden. She walked past the painted flats that vibrated with her tread in her heeled shoes; she stepped over coils of cable, and struts and braces, breathing the smell of paint and canvas and dust and rosin and powder. The smell of powder hung about the dressing-rooms with the smell of cream and grease-paint and gauze from the pupils' dresses hung, wide-skirted ghosts, along their racks; she touched them, and they swung back in a ghost of dancing. She picked up a velvet bow from the floor, and two bus tickets. She took a hand-glass off a stool and blew powder off its glass and put it back on the long dressing-table, where there were tufts of cotton-wool stained with red and blue and flesh-coloured grease-paint, an eyebrow pencil left out; one of the blue skull-caps belonging to the Pages in the *Noble Life* was there, with pins, hair-clips, a piece of a wafer biscuit, and a mascot panda bear. How untidy they are, said Madame. I give them waste-paper baskets, not? She dropped the wafer and the bus tickets and the cotton-wool into a basket and took a shoe off the section of the table next the door. It is bad luck to put shoes on the table, she thought, or is it only new shoes? She hoped it was only new shoes.

She turned out the light and went into the passage where small cubicles made Lion's and Caroline's dressing-rooms opposite each other. Caroline's was immaculate. Well, it should be. She has a dresser, not? It smelled faintly of Caroline's scent. There was an organdie cover on the table and a jar of white lilac. The Lady's dress hung on its hanger, the head-dress was on the table, the shoes on their own rack. Madame went in and touched the fur on the sleeves of the dress. Mine was ermine, she thought. We could not do that for Caroline.

"Let me take it off yours, Madame," Zanny had said, but she would not let her dress be touched.

"But, Anna, you don't want it."

"I do," said Madame.

"But . . ."

"I am going to be buried in it," snapped Madame.

Now it seemed to her cheap and pitiful that Caroline's ermine should be white rabbit fur sewn with black. "It looks as good from the front," said Zanny. That was the whole point, of course, and Madame concurred in it, but it still seemed to her cheap. She still did not think it could be the same. "It is a question of quality," she said. The quality was gone. It was that back-drop in *Carnaval* over again. "And I shall not give *Carnaval* till I can have them," said Madame. That might be the wrong point of view, but it was Madame's.

"Hilda ought to have a dressing-room," Miss Ilse had said.

"Has she said so?" demanded Madame.

"No, but . . . she is a principal."

"And what about Liuba?"

"Hilda is rather more than Liuba. She isn't just a principal."

"There is no dressing-room. She will have to share and share alike. It won't hurrt her. Why shouldn't she?"

Miss Ilse did not answer, but it seemed to her that Hilda was not alike. Sometimes, she thought, Anna is curiously ungrateful.

On Lion's door was a small brass knocker of a lion's head with a ring in its mouth. They put rings in animal noses so that they can be led, thought Madame irrelevantly . . . but the ring was in the lion's mouth. The dressing-rooms were so close to the stage that a rule of silence had to be kept; someone had tied up the lion's mouth with a piece of silk.

Madame put out the lights and went back into the theatre and through it to the foyer. It was close here and smelled of print and paper. She looked at the booking plans on the ledge of the little box-office. They were full for almost the whole season. She touched the telephone, silent now, but it, like the one in the office, had been ringing all day. The lettering on the handbills was clear and large. *Cat Among the Pigeons. The Noble Life. Lyre with Seven Strings.* "Tchk-tchk!" said Madame.

There were photographs along the walls, chiefly of Lion, and Caroline, but also of Rayevskaya, Hilda, John, Francis, Lippi, Alma. On a stand was a large one of Madame as the Humming-Bird in Buenos Aires sixty years ago and, in the corner of the frame, a small one of Archie. Madame had half a mind to take Archie out. There were others of Madame in *Lac des Cygnes, Schéhérazade, Giselle, Snowflakes, Thamar,* as the Princess Aurora, as the Lady. Tomorrow the whole foyer would be heaped with flowers. "They are sure to send me flowers," said Madame.

Emile had swept the carpet here before he went to bed. Its crimson glowed deep and clear against the white walls and gilt frames. It oll looks charming, thought Madame. Just as I should have it look. She looked up at the chandelier and smiled. Its crystal caught the light in its drops and reflected the crimson and white and gleams of gold. I was rright about the chandelier, said Madame.

She turned out the lights here too and went back into the theatre, and at last put out the last light and stood at the garden door looking back into the dark cave of the auditorium, so small compared to any other she had known but, tonight and tomorrow night, much more important. The light from outside, cast into the garden from the street lamps on the pavements, showed a patch of cream wall, the backs of a few rows of seats, a candle sconce. They waited.

Lion had said, "Wait till tomorrow. You never know."

"Something olways saves me at the eleventh minute, not?" Madame said that often, but now she could not think as far as that; she only caught, like a breath from the theatre, what Lion had said, "Wait. Wait till tomorrow."

She stepped outside into the garden and closed the door.

Chapter Four

MADAME went upstairs and found Miss Ilse in her bedroom, where she had been feeling the bottle Zanny had put in Madame's bed to see if it were really hot. She thought Madame was Zanny and jumped. "Anna, how late you are! It's very late."

"Where were you? You olways go away just when I want you. You have been over to the Convent, Ilse. What use are you to me?"

"Only for a moment, and when I came in there was your supper to arrange. Zanny was in the theatre. And there have been notes all day and telephone messages." She looked at Madame. "Anna, has it gone worse? Is it still wrong?"

"No. Not at oll!" said Madame bitingly.

"You are tired out," said Miss Ilse. "You will work your-self to death at this rate, Anna."

"Yes, I will," said Madame. "And what do you care? When I am dead you will be able to go to church and pray for me, oll you like, and I shall be wiped out, oll I have done

. . . and not done," said Madame. "That is oll you care. Oll!"

"God forgive you, Anna," said Miss Ilse. "You are very unjust." Her voice was trembling. "Your supper is ready in the sitting-room. I am going to bed."

Madame let her go. She went to the window and looked down on the road.

Outside, the last bus had run, the road was empty, the street lamps shed a pool of light on empty pavements. The trees rustled. The wind had again that scent of flowers that Hilda had not noticed. Madame noticed it; it was the town cousin of a country wind. She did not remember a London night as quiet, with this night wind and scent. It gave her a nostalgia but she did not know for what, for whom. She said, forgetting Miss Ilse was not there, "Ilse, do you remember the nightingale?"

Miss Ilse could not remember the nightingale. The nightingale was before Miss Ilse, before even she, Madame, had become Anna Holbein, when she was a child and lived in her grandmother's house in the country, a child called Niura. *Listen, Niura, that is a nightingale.* She remembered the words but not who had spoken them, nor, no matter how she trained her ears, could she hear the least thread of song and surely one should remember, first, its song of a nightingale?

"You always were unpredictable, irresponsible, Anna." Miss Ilse had said that, but it was only half true. Unpredictable, yes, but not irresponsible. Tonight her shoulders were bowed with it; she was old, old in responsibility. Old, but what I was I am forever, said Madame. I am still Niura who heard the nightingale.

She went into the sitting-room, familiar with its colours and comfort and warmth but unfamiliar, too, tonight as if she saw it for the first time. Whom does this belong to? . . . It did not belong to Niura, the little girl. It was too rich for her. . . . You have to get used to this rrichness gradually or it will give you indigestion, said Madame. She shivered. Indigestion? Ilse is right. I need food.

The fire was bright. In front of it, drawn up to it, was a small table with a white lace-edged cloth. It was set for supper and with candles in a two-branched gilt candlestick. Like a little altar, thought Madame. Ilse knows I love candlelight. It was an altar. In all the quarrels in the world Miss Ilse would still consecrate herself to see that Madame had her supper. She must have come in, just before, to light the candles. I should go to her, said Madame, but she did not go.

She sat down by the fire. There was a tumbler with red wine in it, and, balanced across it, a spoon with a lump of sugar; beside it was a hot-water jug wrapped round in a napkin. As Madame lifted its lid, steam came out. She poured in the water and dropped the sugar in and sat stirring it round. Such horrible wine, thought Madame, making a grimace; but Miss Ilse thought it was good for her and put it out for her every evening. It was at any rate warm and comforting. She sat holding it, watching the sugar turn dark. I don't remember my grandmother, thought Madame, but I remember her black skirt turned back from the fire as she sat like this and I remember the glass in her hand and the spoon stirring and the sugar turning dark. What she did I do now, thought Madame. I must be very old.

The house, that house, was wooden with slats and a birch tree at the gate. She remembered the birch leaves in spring, and the gate made a noise, *ouoie-ouoiee-eee*, because its wood had swelled. There was a flat place along the road where there were other trees. Willows, said Madame. . . . In the summer the dust in the road was white, she could feel it between her bare toes, and the frogs croaked all night; unlike the nightingale, she could hear the frogs. Yes, there were frogs and tadpoles and a boy, thought Madame. Nikita? Vaslav? Stanislav? She could not remember his name.

She lifted the dish cover and began her supper; it was one of Zanny's ragouts with a chicken, a few button mushrooms, and very small carrots. She must have made it before Ilse got there. I am glad she did, thought Madame. Zanny, who cooked untidily, was a far better cook than Miss Ilse. "But she isn't clean, Anna. Food should be pure." "I don't like my food pure," said Madame, "I like it to *taste*." Miss Ilse had added brown bread and butter, a salad, and strawberries and cream. Madame left the salad, she knew Miss Ilse's salads, and ate the rest. . . . But she arranged oll this for me and what did she have herself? . . .

Nothing. Tea and bread and butter. Care and devotion. Madame sighed. Tonight she did not want care and devotion, she wanted judgment. Someone who could judge for her or help her to judge for herself. That is what I didn't have, thought Madame. No judgment. None at oll. Never. Or did I? she asked. Thinking over her life, backwards, down the years, it seemed to her that she did. She could not possibly have managed as well as she did, without.

It was curious how totally she had forgotten Niura and how refreshing she found it, in her tiredness, to remember her now. There was a river, she thought eating her supper, and there, as well as the frogs and the tadpoles, there was a crane. These things were like footfalls in her memory, she could follow them where they led; she saw the crane now, standing in the water on one leg. But it couldn't have done that oll the time, she argued, but that was how Niura had seen it and for her it stood like that for ever. As she had remembered the feel of the summer dust in the road between her toes, she remembered paddling in the river; she saw her feet, through the water, on the river sand. They look quite ordinary feet, thought Madame, the feet of any little girl, but they were mine. That was the miracle. That one pair of feet should have a power denied to another, that all feet were the same, and all different.

She tried to take herself one step further, where Niura had gone away with Jan, the big brother come from their father's relations in Holland; Jan had taught her there in the country all one summer . . . and I didn't like it. I wept.

He was so stern, said Madame, and then he took me away and I wasn't Niura, I was Anna, and then we came back to St. Petersburg and I went to the Maryinsky school. . . . *Among the small pupils that year was the little Anna Holbein,* a great ballerina had written in her memoirs. *I remember the fragile big-eyed little girl with the grasshopper legs, as we used to call them. She was surprisingly naughty. Perhaps no one had ever dared to be naughty there before. We were always surprised when she was forgiven. Looking back on her now, I am no longer surprised. She was extraordinarily gifted. I remember her . . .*

Madame could not remember her at all. Instead, into her mind came Lollie. But she is not at oll like I was, said Madame. I never had plaits turned up in those knobs! Nor that woe-begone smile, she might have added, nor that name. What a name! said Madame. No one has a name like that. She will have to use another, said Madame.

"When you were my age," Lollie asked her, "were you much better than me?"

"Than 'I,' Lollie."

"But were you? Were you?"

Madame could not see the small Anna for Lollie. She could clearly see her grandmother's house with its birch trees and the wooden gate; she could see the birds and tadpoles Niura had been interested in . . . and how lucky I was to have that childhood, thought Madame. How much came out of it later.

"I have never seen the wind in a field of corn."

Madame sighed and put away her plate and took a strawberry. Stars, to Lollie, might easily mean film stars . . . and yet, she *should* have seen stars, argued Madame, on the top of a bus, for instance . . . but it would only be from the top of a bus, not on a hill, open above woods, or through trees, or in a foreign train, crossing the plain like a little glittering snake under the glittering sky, or in the mountains where a peak could shut off a whole galaxy of stars, or on a ship made small by its own loneliness between the wide sky and sea. But one day she will see it, thought Madame. Even for Lollie, if she works and has a little luck, it may be. There will be nothing phenomenal in that, it would be purely natural. It always annoyed her when they said her own success was phenomenal. "It was not in the least," she said. "It was only to be expected." I must do more for Lollie, she thought now. More for oll of them. But she knew she could not. Each must get on as best he might.

She rolled a strawberry in sugar. "Not too much sugar, Anna. We have to be careful . . ." "Don't you dole my sugar to me," said Madame. "Let me enjoy it and then, if there is no more, I shall do without. That is the way to live," said Madame severely. Miss Ilse sighed. Madame made such an issue of little things. "But little things are the issue," said Madame. "They are the same as big."

Now she dipped the strawberry whole in sugar and ate it thoughtfully, slowly, looking into the fire. The summer scents of that garden were not like their town cousin she had smelled from her window tonight; they were robust and rough but fragrant; she remembered hay-making days, and poppies and marguerites growing in the rye, the corn Lollie had never seen. Marguerites. Marguerites always made Madame think of *Giselle*. Of all ballets *Giselle* was unquestionably the one she loved the most. I had marguerites for it once, marguerites with the white gauze. They said they were not correct, but I think they suited it better than lilies or roses. Marguerites; those grave-eyed flowers. There is a photograph of me with them, thought Madame. I must get Ilse to change it for the one in the foyer. I should like to have it there tomorrow night. *Giselle* . . . in the second act, with Albrecht . . . and suddenly she found that she was not thinking of the young Anna Holbein; she was thinking of Hilda. "Tchk-tchk!" said Madame, and pushed the strawberries away.

Why should she think of Hilda? It was not likely that Hilda would ever dance *Giselle*. How many dancers do? Few in each generation. Then I can safely prophesy . . . But can anyone safely prophesy anything? Prophets can, perhaps, but Madame was no prophet. But I don't think she will go as far as that, said Madame.

She thought of the way she herself had come since the days of Niura. It seemed to her like a road winding and winding, round loops and bends and corners and up steep places with precipices and chasms and barriers to make it difficult and longer. And I used to think it would be like a meadow, a panorama meadow with flowers and lawns and a brook to cool it and sun and a blue sky. But it wasn't in the *least,* said Madame.

When she thought of the road, particularly the precipices, she thought of Hilda; when she thought of the meadow, the panorama meadow, she thought of Caroline. Now what is the significance of that? she asked. She felt it had significance, but she did not know what it could be. She was too tired, tired out, too tired to divine. I am no more a witch than a prophet, said Madame crossly. Nor, what do they call it, a delph? A sibyl? She was too tired to think what she was. I am I, I suppose, she said. That seemed to comprehend it all.

The starting point, the freshet, was Lollie. Not Lollie, Niura, she corrected, but, obstinately, it was Lollie. A freshet is a spring, the bubbling, rising, of a spring. Spring. Even while there were snowdrifts, snowdrops—no, snow-drifts—on the ground, the spring wind used to blow in the birch trees. . . . Birch buds, you should make tea of them and drink it in the spring; it makes old blood young again. But that isn't possible, said Madame. I have been through oll the seasons, said Madame. This season, that season; but now it is only winter, winter alone, without a trrace of spring. I am in winter now . . . and she shivered. Why am I shivering? I have my food and my *vin sucré.* I shouldn't be cold. But I am cold. Cold. She drew her chair closer to the fire. I must expect to be cold, said Madame, to feel the frost in me, to be bound and cold as ice. I can't expect to be arrdent, and eager as I was as a young girl, though even now I am more arrdent than most of them, said Madame with a flicker of her self; but the flicker sank down. It is too difficult to be ardent when one is tired. Too tiring, said Madame. You can't make old blood young again.

She thought of herself in the photograph downstairs, that young girl with the ringlets, and other early photographs: the one with the marguerites that was to go into the foyer, the Odile in the black tutu she had innovated, in *Armide*, in *Thamar* . . . all with the same grace of arms and neck and head, the straight beauty of the legs, the face with its iridescent eyes . . . oll me, thought Madame, and found again that she was thinking of Hilda.

This . . . this double memory, cried Madame. Life was exceedingly treacherous. Alone? Alone in winter? Nothing was alone, by itself. She could not remember in peace any more than she could be angry in peace. Everything, every-one, everything, insisted on being with something or some-body else. When she wished to think about herself, she thought of these Lollies and Hildas. It was provoking. And why think of Hilda, when it is Caroline I love? The thought of Caroline gave her a stab. How little she cared for you tonight, it said. Madame lifted her chin. If you love people, you must be prepared to suffer them. I shall speak to Car-oline in the morning, said Madame. I shall speak to her privately as I couldn't do with oll of them there in the theatre. She will take it from me. Caroline is olways sweet-tempered, and it is naturral she should get swollen head, not? The wonder is that it hasn't happened before. I shall speak in the morning and it will be oll rright, but Hilda . . . That brought her back to the trouble of the ballet. It isn't oll right, cried Madame in despair. Hilda. Why did I ever see Hilda? It is a fiasco. A fiasco!

Never before, said Madame, have I had nothing new to show; nothing to make them talk, worth while to remember. A young dancer, a new ballet, a new idea. A nest-egg of ballet, said Madame bitterly, with not one single egg in it! Nothing to show. Nothing to bring them to see, only the old, with no new blood in it. Adequate? Ah yes, of course, but that is oll, and it isn't even adequate with a third of the programme gone. Ah, why did I listen to Felix? Why did I listen to Lion? Why didn't I use my own judgment, if I had any judgment, thought Madame.

It was very quiet. Time seemed to be suspended in the house, but, if she listened, she could hear the clocks ticking, her Swiss clock that she had bought not in Switzerland but in New York and her Dresden clock that she had bought not in Dresden but in Paris. They had begun to tick in Berne and Dresden as they ticked here, now, in London; as they had ticked in Paris and New York and all over the world: London, Paris, Dresden, Berlin, St. Petersburg, Petrograd, Milan, Madrid, Johannesburg, Cape Town, Sydney, Adelaide, Brisbane, Buenos Aires, Rio, San Francisco, New York. She saw the labels that were pasted to the slips on the dress baskets. She saw Miss Ilse pasting them freshly on again and again, pinkish labels printed *Ballet Holbein* in large letters; Royal Theatre, Copenhagen: La Scala, Milan:

the Colon, Buenos Aires: Zarzuela, Madrid: Civic Opera House, Chicago. Oll over the world, said Madame. And not for one performance, one, have I failed. That is a record, I think, said Madame. . . . That success had not been easy, it was often tedious, troublesome, with bone-breaking work. They forget the work, said Madame. Well, let them. The work is nothing, but . . . even to work isn't enough. One can fail. Ah, what shall I do? What shall I do? said Madame.

Hilda! Hilda! Hilda! ticked the clocks. Time passes, but that is what it doesn't do, said Madame, it goes on and on for ever. You cannot get away from it. She leaned back in her chair and closed her eyes.

Listen, Niura. That is a nightingale.

She could not remember the name of that boy. There were others. There was Serge and Paul. She had not thought of them for a long time. And that French boy, Jean Marie. I called him Médor, he was like a faithful little dog to me. There was that young Englishman, Gerald . . . Gerald? Well, Gerald, said Madame. . . . There was Kuprin, her first partner, and into her mind came a strange old Scotsman who had followed her last tour all through South America, from place to place, never speaking to anyone in the company, never writing or asking to meet her, but always in the theatre to see her dance; I used to bow to him, thought Madame, but he never sent me any flowers. I suppose he thought he had spent enough in following us about, and it must have cost him a good deal, thought Madame fairly. It had made her remember him, that he had never sent her flowers. There had been so many flowers. She remembered the bouquet that had been in the little holder upstairs, the bouquet with the lace frill. . . . It was after the accident in Copenhagen. Ilse said he would drive fast and he did. . . . Like Miss Ilse, she could remember his moustache, but she could not remember his name. She remembered the gala performance, *Swan Lake*. She remembered kissing the Queen's hand in its white glove and she remembered the bouquet. They had stiffened its lace and that had shocked Miss Ilse. She had washed it lovingly. . . . I have it still in the cabinet on the stairs.

Yes. There were many who had loved Anna Holbein, but whom had she loved? I suppose I loved them, thought Madame. Perhaps I loved them oll—or none. A flame came up from the glow of the coals and shone, reflected in the polish of the chairs and tables, in the glass and silver on the table, in the candlestick, in the mirrors and on the walls.

Anna. My darling. Darling Anna.

Yes, they said that, said Madame, nodding her head, they felt it . . . and what was one to do when one felt that rush of love? That mastery? What was one to do against that power? Nothing at oll, said Madame. Why make such a fuss of it? Miss Ilse, for instance, always made a fuss. You would think it the ends of the earth, said Madame. "Anna, you should be *ashamed*," Miss Ilse had said. "I am not ashamed," said Madame mildly.

Anna. Darling Anna. They were only words . . .

and it is a parrt of life, not? said Madame, those words?

The first season she gave *The Noble Life* . . . It is because we do it now that I think of him, because I am tired,
but . . . She could not remember him, clearly. It had not
been for long, a few weeks from a lifetime, but she should
not have forgotten them; she wanted to remember them
now. In the morning, before it was really morning, while
it was still night, when the first light lay in the angle of
the window frames, and the bird song had begun in the
garden. *"To hold your hands is like holding two birds in
my hands, Anna." "You are thinking of the birds in the
garden." "Are they birds, that sleepy noise?"* She was almost
with him, then instead she saw Lion.

She thought of Lion. Of Lion's golden skin with olive
lights, of his hair that was crinkled with curls like the pelt
of a lamb, of his eyes. She saw him in his silks and velvets
as the Nobleman, in his street clothes, in his dark tights.
I had lovers, said Madame. Yes. Well? I needed a counterpart. Just as I had to have a partner in the dance. That was
oll. No more than that. I was olways busy. I could not give
myself away. No, I could not do that. . . . Well, Lion is
not for me, she said, but, however firmly she said it, she
felt again that rebellious pang of jealousy. Ah. Don't conflict me so, said Madame to herself. You are old. For years
you have been old. You should be used to it by now, said
Madame severely, and she sighed. It had been peaceful to
be old, till now.

She raised her head and listened. The emptiness of the

house answered her. Even the mice are asleep, said Madame. How did I come to think such thoughts, thoughts that haven't trroubled me for years? But do they trouble me? Ah no! They give me rrest, and joy, thought Madame, leaning back in her chair, and strength.

In the night, she thought, when everyone is asleep, that is the time, when the moments are emptied of the thoughts of others, cleared, that is the time to think. That is why thought comes as strongly and as truly as it has tonight. I have been awake oll night as I was then, said Madame, but afterwards, in the morning, I slept. . . . There was no arm round her now, no shoulder and breast to pillow her head, she was alone, her little tired body upright in the arm-chair. She shut her eyes, but almost at once, indignantly, they opened. She was thinking of Hilda again.

Into her mind had come the remembrance of Hilda dancing with Lion. They could have their perfect moment, those two children, she had thought involuntarily. They are matched. Nonsense, said Madame. Hilda a match for Lion? That is presumption, and she began to be indignant again, then found she was too tired. I can't bother about them. They must get on as best they can, thought Madame. I am too tired to combat them. Lion must fend for himself. I am too tired.

There was no warmth and support or inspiration or glory now for her, and she had none to give. My day is over, said Madame.

She lifted her head. Under the blinds that Miss Ilse had

drawn, the light lay in the angle of the window frames, an angle of light and an angle of darkness, that she had seen before. She could hear the first sound of a chirp in the garden. It isn't night, she said. It is day.

She was reluctant to meet this day. To go into it with its troubles and difficulties and strain and work. I am not fit for it, said Madame. I have had no rest, no sleep, and it will be a calamitous day. I feel it.

Oll over the world and here in London, day after day, year in, year out, what I have done, I have done well, till now. I have been prroud of that, prroud and interested to be proud. I am not interested in failure. I have olways given the best, the very best, said Madame. She looked round bewildered as if she did not know how this had happened, how it was that this day promised her, Madame Holbein, no success. She felt old, beaten, too tired, too cold, to deal with it. Her eyes felt as dry as paper, her body ached. What am I to do? Cancel the season? Put off the performance tonight? Return the seats? How can I? But what else? What else is there to do? I wanted to show them Caroline in a big role, and Caroline doesn't choose to dance. Rayevskaya is charming, but she is nothing, and the ballets are nothing new. As they stand they are not enough. What shall I do?

Have a backbone, not a wishbone, Anna. Who said that? She remembered. It was Jan. "Yes," said Madame aloud. "Yes." Another feeling came up in her, tough and obstinate with pride, and with a certain excitement of its own. Olways, at the eleventh minute, I save myself, said Madame. She pushed back the chair and stood up. I don't know what I shall do, but something. Something, that is what I shall do.

She began to walk about. She had a hot flush on each cheek, and her eyes, under those paper eyelids, felt hard and glittering. I must have deep wrinkles this morning, she thought. The room, with its blinds drawn, the ashes in the fire, and its used supper table, seemed dead and depressing, closed in by the night. She opened the door and listened and went down to the first classrooms where there were no blinds to pull, no curtains to draw and shut out this necessary day. Here she could meet it, as it had to be met.

Someone had left the window open. A wave of cool, dew-filled air met her and, though it chilled her, it was freshening. The garden was empty and colourless, cold and unfeeling. After a moment she pushed the window down; now the garden was a glass garden with no wind and no birds. That is better, said Madame. Better for me today.

She stood looking at the theatre wall, at the door that would presently open. She thought beyond it, into the theatre, the auditorium that would presently be filled with pleasantly expectant people, of Miss Parkes' sister with the programmes, of the orchestra that would assemble, of Mr. Felix, of Glancy and William on the stage, of the busy hive behind it: Rebecca and Miss Parkes scurrying to and fro, Zanny and Miss Porteus, the dancers; beyond them again to the frontage, and the foyer, where the bills were posted and Emile in his blue uniform would wait to open the car doors. Yes, said Madame, and pressed her hands to her temples. Yes. But what to do? What to do?

Here in this room were all the habits of her life and work; all her discipline, her inspiration. She looked around it as if she were calling to it, asking it to rally to her now. The floor, dusty, dry with the lines of its boards; the wainscot, runway of the mice, with its holes and cracks and blistered paint; the embossed old darkened paper; the *barres* in their iron clamps; the piano shut as Mr. Felix left it shut, music on its top, music under the cushion of the stool, and bursting from the rack: the forms under the windows, the white stuffing showing in the splits of their red seats; a pair of shoes left on the floor under them, their tapes trailing in the dirt of the floor; the gramophone. Madame's eyes stopped.

The gramophone was open, its lid raised, and on it was an open notebook. She walked over to it. On the turn-table was a large record; she could not read its label without lifting it up, but she picked up the notebook; the writing was as large, sprawled, and untidy as her own; she could read it without bringing it too close to her eyes. *Solo, Leda,* she read: *Leda travels backwards on line five to centre: entrechat quatre, relevé passé derrière on alternate feet, arms fifth en bas* . . . Leda? asked Madame, and turned the pages back: *Leda, looking for shells on the lake shore* . . . she read. "Tchk-tchk!" said Madame, and she carried the book to the light and read on, stooping her nose into the pages: *And now, towards the reeds and the girl, the Swan comes with a rush, the wings beat round her, making her stagger and reel dizzily, bearing her backwards* . . . "Tchk-tchk!" said Madame.

She turned the book over. In the front was written: *Leda and the Swan*. Hm! said Madame. Now, why did no one ever think of making that into a ballet before? It seemed to her now an inevitable theme. She read the notes through and then went to the gramophone. She took off the record and, holding it close to her eyes, was able to read it: *Fantasia and Variations*, Carlorossi. Never heard of it, said Madame, and put it back again, switched the gramophone on, and released the catch. It began quietly, then the raucous impolite music she had heard in the garden burst into the room. "Tchk-tchk!" cried Madame, recoiling in surprise. "Tchk-tchk-tchk!" but she listened.

There was no hiding that music. It broke its way into every corner of the house and woke Miss Ilse and brought her running down the stairs.

"Anna! What are you doing?" But her voice was drowned in sound.

The music rent the air. Miss Ilse had to wait until it was finished.

"Anna? It's only five o'clock. You will wake the whole road."

"Hush," said Madame.

"Hush. After that noise." She looked at Madame. "Anna, you haven't been to bed all night."

"No," Madame agreed abstractedly. Her voice was buoyant and full of life.

Miss Ilse stared at her. "Anna," she said suspiciously, "what have you been doing?"

"What should I have been doing?" asked Madame, not thinking of her.

"You . . . you look like you used to do," said Miss Ilse. "You look almost like a young girl. Anna, what did you do last night?"

"Last night?" Madame could not remember last night. Last night was over. It was today.

Chapter Five

"ILSE, you must get Lion."

"Lion? *Now?* Do you know what the time is, Anna?"

"Yes, you have told me," said Madame, and she said urgently, "There isn't a minute to lose. And Felix. You must get Felix."

"But, Anna . . ."

"And Edwin for lights, and who . . . who for the set? Mathilde? No. Noel for this, but I suppose he has only gone to bed; no, better not Noel perhaps. He is bad-tempered in the morning, and we can't wait. Pierre Moron, perhaps. But no. No. Noel is better; wake Zanny; and Miss Porteus, we shall have to get Miss Porteus . . ."

"But, Anna . . ."

"But nothing can be done without Lion." She turned on Miss Ilse. "Why are you standing there, not even dressed? Why are you waiting? I said you should get Lion. Then get Lion, at once."

"But how shall I get him? He will be in bed. They will all be in bed. No one will answer the telephone."

"Then you must go in a taxi and fetch him."

"Where shall I get a taxi at five in the morning?" Miss Ilse dissolved into tears. "You are so unfeeling, Anna. Last night and now . . . this morning. I don't understand what is happening," sobbed Miss Ilse. "You haven't been to bed all night. You look as if you had been . . . I don't understand. I don't understand what is happening. How do you expect me to understand when you don't explain?"

Madame had a moment of exasperation, then she came and put her arms round Miss Ilse. "Do you remember the time when you went to Milan and fetched my shoes?" she asked, her cheek against Miss Ilse's pale wet one. "It was just at the opening of the Covent Garden season and Baretti had sent my shoes and sent them oll wrrong? I was in despair, remember?"

Miss Ilse nodded. She remembered the despair very well.

"And you went strraight to Milan to get them. No one else but you would have gone."

"There was no one else to go," said Miss Ilse, but she sniffed back her tears.

"There is no one else now," said Madame. "There never has been. You know that, Ilse. You have olways helped me. You must help me now. I haven't time to explain to you more than this: I think I have discovered something that may . . . only may . . . Ilse, solve us for the perrformance tonight. If I have, it will save us from disgrace," said Madame dramatically.

"Is it as bad as that, Anna?"

"Well, no," admitted Madame, "but any fall at our height would be hard to bear, Ilse, not? Everyone would be sorry we were not as good. They would rregret. I refuse to have regrrets. Last night I was wretched. I didn't see how it could be saved, and now I have found, what do you think? A new ballet, Ilse."

"A new ballet! Now! Oh, *Anna!*"

"Don't say 'Oh,' say 'Ah,' " said Madame testily. " 'Ah' is big, dramatic, generous . . ."

"But everyone says 'Oh'!"

"Yes, everyone! Ilse, it isn't a ballet, not a complete . . . but I think it *is* complete, and it's more than a dance. It is a ballet, a ballet for two." She paused and went over to the gramophone and picked up the notebook and brought it to Miss Ilse. "Ilse, this book is Hilda's, not? It's her writing."

Miss Ilse, her head in a maze, was able to say that it was.

"It would be!" said Madame.

"Mother of God, a new ballet!" Miss Ilse was praying. "*Now!* Mother of God, Mary, help us. It isn't possible, but she will make it possible. Oh, help us. Give us strength." Panic broke through. "How is it possible?" cried Miss Ilse. "There are only a few hours before the curtain goes up. Who is to dance it, Anna? Learn it, rehearse it in the time? It isn't possible."

"It is," said Madame.

"And it isn't only the rehearsing. There is music. Dresses. Lights. And what will you do for a set? Use curtains . . ."

"You know I never use curtains."

"But you will have to . . ."

"I shan't."

"But . . ."

"Ah, Ilse, don't make me such a storrm in a teapot. We shall never get on."

"And the programmes will have to be altered. What about the *printers?*" cried Miss Ilse.

"Ilse, I beg of you. Before I lose my temper," said Madame blazing, "go and get me Lion."

Lion came.

"I know about it," said Lion. He looked sideways at Madame. "It was that that I was dancing with Hilda when you stopped us yesterday."

"It was that? Why didn't you tell me?" She gave him no time to answer but swept on, looking at him intently. "How good is it, Lion? Is it good?"

"I think so," said Lion.

"Why didn't you tell me about it instead of about that *Lyre?*"

"I didn't know what it was until I danced it with Hilda last night."

"And last night I was in despair and you knew and you still didn't tell me." She stopped. "You wanted it for the Metropolitan, Lion."

"I didn't." Lion flushed.

"You did."

"It never occurred to me."

"You are oll, oll the same," said Madame with scorn. *There is an infinite variety in people.* Who had said that? My mind is full of ends and tags, said Madame, and it's not trrue. There is no variety in people. They are oll the same; oll how do you say it, *clay.* "I don't know what to make of you, Lion," she said sadly.

"No, you don't." Lion was surly and offended.

I don't know in the least if he did it or not, thought Madame. No. I don't know what to make of Lion.

"The Metropolitan is my company," said Lion sourly.

"So is this."

"That must come first."

"This was first."

"I am sorry you should think this of me."

"So am I."

Madame felt angry and hurt and uncertain. There seemed a hiatus that she could not bridge. She looked at Lion helplessly. Lion walked away to the window and whistled. He doesn't seem to care what I think, said Madame, perplexed. What is the matter with him?

"Anna, you want some breakfast," said Miss Ilse.

"No."

"Some good hot coffee . . ." said Miss Ilse, moving towards the door.

"No."

"And you too, Lion. With toast and some fruit . . ."

"No," said Lion.

"You will feel better for it, both of you. Dear goodness,

Anna was up all night. Nothing to eat . . . enough to make her ill. I will go and get it at once. You will be better after some breakfast."

Miss Ilse could almost have followed her own loved St. Catherine who lived on salads and water, but Madame had to have food; she liked it and needed it and ate it. "A dancer works on her stomach," she often said that, and, though she did not dance, she was still a dancer. It was almost mortifying to see how much better she felt after the coffee and toast and fruit. "And so does Lion," said Madame. "He isn't nearly as quarrelsome, not?"

"And now," said Miss Ilse content, "I can go and call Mr. Felix and then I shall go on for Miss Porteus and Edwin."

Some people *are* different, said Madame, touched. There are a few, a faithful few, who burn like those altar lamps that never go out, that are olways lit by care and devotion. My supper table was like an altar last night. A lamp olways lit, steady, because it is tended. It is devotion that tends them, not like fitful candles, said Madame looking suspiciously at Lion again. "Ilse . . ." she said with love. Then her tone changed. *"Ilse!"*

Miss Ilse had not gone to fetch Mr. Felix. She was standing just outside the door, her face rapt, her eyes shut, her lips moving.

"Ding. Ding-dong," went the Convent bell. It was the Angelus.

"Hail Mary, full of grace . . ."

"Ilse, must you spend time now?"

No answer.

"Ilse would pray when Jericho was falling!" said Madame.

"That would be the time to pray, wouldn't it?" said Lion.

"You must see Hilda before you do anything further," said Lion. "You can't arrange all this without her. You must wait till she comes."

" 'Must,' Lion?"

"Yes, you must."

"Why?"

"Because it's hers."

"She did it in my school, as a member of my company," argued Madame. "What could she possibly have to say?"

"You may not like it when you see it danced."

"I may not. What else?"

"She may not want you to do it." Madame's head came up. "She didn't particularly like the way you treated her over *Lyre*," said Lion.

"Treated her over *Lyre!* To give her a wonderful chance like that! It was a chance even if it didn't happen," said Madame.

"She may prefer the Metropolitan to do it," said Lion smoothly.

"You wouldn't think of it, Lion!"

"You said I would," Lion reminded her.

"Hilda wouldn't trreat me like that. She wouldn't dare.

I shouldn't allow her to trreat me like that—nor you, Lion."
She said again, "Hilda wouldn't treat me like that." Then
she remembered how she had sometimes treated Hilda and
was silenced. Oll these birrds come home to roost, she
thought angrily. It was, she felt, exactly like Hilda to come
home to roost. She paused. "Lion," she said slowly, "Hilda
will want to dance Leda herself."

"Who else?" said Lion. "Or do you want her to give it
to Caroline? I had better go and fetch Hilda. I have a taxi
outside. Zanny is giving the man some breakfast to keep
him quiet."

Madame did not answer. She felt as she had felt about
the Lady. She did not want to relinquish this part to anyone. Relinquish, cried Madame to herself. I have never had
it. If she had to . . . to give it up! thought Madame—
and, in spite of sense, she felt she gave it up—then she
could bear only to give it up to Caroline, and yet . . .
Hilda dancing it was more herself. But I am talking about
the Lady, thought Madame. This is another part. Ah, I
hate to be old! she cried suddenly, silently. I hate to be
old! Where had that feeling come from? She had gone past
that long ago, past the age of regrets. I should have died
before them oll, thought Madame. That is what a dancer
should do, die young. I am old, dried, hideous. And the
whole of her cried again, I don't want anyone else to have
this part.

"Anyway, Leda doesn't matter," said Lion. "She is only
a counterpart to the Swan."

"How can you?" said Madame, up in arms, but Lion only smiled at her quite certainly and went away to fetch Hilda.

This is doing something to Lion, thought Madame, looking after him. Something he needs. He is . . . emerging, said Madame. But is he hard enough, strange enough, for this Swan? It is a strange wild white part. It is bird ferocity, less male, more cruel, than an animal. *The Swan comes with a rush,* a rush of love, said Madame. Lion doesn't know that—or does he? With all her knowledge of him, that was something she could not know; the intimate, the strongest moment is hidden except from one . . . And I am not that one, said Madame, and again she had the feeling of being ousted. "You live on in these children," they said to her. Yes, that is the trrouble, said Madame. I only live in them, and it isn't enough. The old feelings had woken. Ah, don't be so trroublesome, said Madame to herself. There is too much to do for me to be trroubled with you now.

Bring together the component parts . . . but if the parts are in conflict, how will they ever compound? "They must compound," said Madame. The conflict began with Hilda.

"You mean . . . you want to have my *Leda and the Swan* if you like it, instead of *Lyre with Seven Strings?*"

"Of course. Of course," said Madame impatiently. "It is oll settled long ago." It annoyed her that Hilda looked startled.

"How can it be long ago, when I saw you late last night

and it is only seven o'clock in the morning now?" Hilda's look seemed to say.

"I shall explain it to you later," said Madame haughtily. Hilda knew she never would, but she let it pass. "That isn't the point. The point is *time,* dearr child," said Madame. "Lion is changing. Go and get into your practice things and come back to me here and let me see it."

"Then . . . you think *Leda and the Swan* is good?"

Is she doing this on purpose? thought Madame. "Why should it be . . ." she began aloud, and stopped. "How do I know what it is?" she said instead. "I haven't seen it yet."

"But you like the idea?"

"The idea has possibilities," said Madame as judiciously as she could, then her impatience broke. "Well, what are you waiting for?" she cried. "What more do you want?"

"I'm not sure," said Hilda, and another look came into her face. Madame recognized it. She had seen it on many faces before. It had the beginnings of obstinacy; it was wary and she saw it with irritation and a slight sinking of her heart. Surely, she thought, I shall not have to *flatter* this out of Hilda. That would be too . . . Ah! How can clever people be so stupid! asked Madame impatiently, but she knew quite well they could.

"Listen to me, dearr child," she said, and, all the while, the precious minutes were ticking away. We shall never get done at this rate, thought Madame, and aloud: "Listen to me." She had no idea what she had to say to which Hilda could profitably listen, but she knew it was no use arguing; the more one argued with that look the more embattled it became, but "Listen to me," she said. Inspiration came. "Hilda, it was many years ago Mikhail Mikhailovitch came to my dressing-room . . ."

Hilda's unabated look asked plainly what Mikhail Mikhailovitch was to do with her.

"Mikhail was Mayakovsky, the manager. He came to my dressing-room and he said, 'Anna. Go to Signora Beltrametti and get fitted for Tanya's dress and then go on the stage to Polonsky. You will dance the Doll tonight.' He did not explain to me: Tanya has quarrelled with Polonsky, they have refused to dance together, and I have refused her to stay without it, and such-and-such an arrangement has been made. No. There was no need to. I accepted it without a worrd," said Madame. Lion had come in and she saw him look at her, in that new sideways way. "Without a murmur," said Madame defiantly at Lion. "And that was my success, Hilda. I was second ballerina then, it was trrue; perhaps our cases are not parallel, but after that I was second to nobody, *but* if I had quarrelled and quibbled I should not have had my destiny." She put her hand gently on Hilda's shoulder. "Is this perhaps your destiny, Hilda?" she asked.

Was destiny too large a word to use to Hilda? No, destinies can be oll sizes, said Madame.

Hilda had several things she meant to say to Madame: Are you going to change it and twist it and spoil it? Will you pull this one to pieces too? Is it going to be my ballet or yours? . . . Now she went to change without a word.

"Did Mikhail Mikhailovitch come to your dressing-room?" asked Lion when Hilda had gone.

"Of course he did," said Madame, and with dignity she asked, "Why not?"

"I wondered," said Lion smoothly.

"You can't manage people with lies, my dear Lion," said Madame untruthfully, and added, "At least, not for very long."

Hilda, when she came back again, looked as if she were destined for beauty. That is only an illusion, said Madame. She isn't at oll beautiful. Her face is too narrow, her neck is too long, but what has happened to her? thought Madame.

Hilda had not chosen to put on her usual practice dress. With tights, she wore a white tutu and, because it was early and cold, she had wound her bodice and shoulders with an old scarf of poppy-coloured silk sewn with sequins. As she came in, with her sleek small head and scintillating scarf and fine legs in their tights and ribbon-laced shoes, she had a springing radiant vitality that surprised Madame. I seem to be continually surprised at Hilda, she thought, as if she has a fund of life to draw on. But that is what I had, thought Madame jealously. Hilda's eyes were radiant, her skin fresh . . . as dew, thought Madame. That is because she is young . . . and her jealousy grew more biting. "Why a tutu?" asked Madame. "It should have been a tunic for Leda."

Hilda stared at her rebuked. It should have been a tunic for Leda. At this important minute she, Hilda, had been thinking not of Leda, the role, but of herself. That was unlike Hilda. Madame looked at her curiously as she went across the floor and stood in Leda's first pose, waiting for Lion to release the gramophone and set the needle. As she took the pose, Madame saw her smile at Lion. Hilda thought the smile was secret, but it was completely palpable to Madame. She has been kissed in the taxi, that one, said Madame.

Lion set the needle and the music began. *Leda, looking for shells on the lake shore* . . .

Because Madame had liked the theme of the ballet, because it appealed to her, perhaps peculiarly appealed to her, she watched it all the more severely. She would not be betrayed again into overlooking anything . . . no, not even by my personal taste. . . . To be impersonal is to be dull, to be too personal is to make judgment difficult, and Madame, for all her doubts and lapses, still knew how to judge. She stood, a stern scrutator, watching Lion and Hilda dance.

There was no help in the room. The light was bleak and cold, they were in practice dress, though Hilda had the warm colour of the scarf; the room was too small, the music sounded too loud and blatant in its narrow space, and Madame was in no mood to be pleased; she was tired in mind and body, she ached from her eyes to her insteps, and she had a pain in the back of her neck and in her temples that felt stiff and taut with strain. She watched intently. They had several stops; places where Hilda had to stop Lion and explain to him, or read directions; they stopped again and then again. Hilda threw a quick look at Madame, but Madame remained patient. Presently it took shape. They went back to the beginning and it began to move; it moved swiftly. One of the things Madame saw and noted with approval was its pace. Older people, many older, will envy that, she found herself thinking. Where did she get it from? asked Madame.

Choreography, the science and design of dancing, is not to be arrived at easily, in five minutes, or five years, or, for most, not in fifty. How then had this young silent girl achieved it? Madame did not know, but she saw, as the pattern of the ballet unfolded, how deep and firm were the strata of Hilda's knowledge. And so they should be, said Madame. I taught her . . . but she knew that few, perhaps none, of the others had learnt from her like this. Hilda had something Madame had not taught her, and had it in more degree than Madame herself. She had vision. *She knows more than she knows she knows.* Who had said that? Mr. Felix. Felix, said Madame. Felix will say *I told you so.* And he will be right, said Madame.

The ballet was short and as tense and dramatic as even Madame could have wished. Leda, the young unconscious dreaming virgin Leda, is attacked on the lake shore by the

Swan in all his force; then in his preening solitary love dance he dances alone until, under his renewed savage force, Leda abandons herself and is carried away. It was an extravagant theme, but Hilda had discarded extravagance; it had no virtuoso, no extravagant lifts or fireworks such as might be expected with the strength of the theme and her slight experience. It had technical strength and it had drama. And it has beauty, said Madame, and she paused. It makes you remember it after . . . said Madame. It's bold, she said, very bold for a young girl's work, and strong. No wonder I felt her too strong in the classroom. And she looked at Hilda with that surprise again. It's a long time since I saw a ballet that is romantic without nostalgia, said Madame. As if romance must be half dead, not? This is alive, said Madame. I feel it, my pulses feel it. I didn't know I had such pulses, said Madame.

Lion and Hilda stood shoulder to shoulder, their cheeks hot and their eyes bright, waiting for Madame's verdict. Her excitement had communicated itself to them as theirs had to her. She said, "Dance it again."

They danced and, watching them then, Madame thought they were never again to dance it quite as they did this time. They were excited, and their feeling for one another was in its first flush and so, after all, was the ballet in its first flush. Afterwards must come the toil of its production when it would become real with properties attached to it; when, built up round its first conception, must come buttresses of *décor,* orchestration, dresses, lights. Now it was itself, still visionary though fledged. I should like it to stay like that, said Madame, though she had no intention of allowing it. I wish it could keep that . . . that pristine quality, but they don't. They don't because they can't; they can't be new again for ever . . . or only a few—a very few. It isn't to be supposed that this is one of the few, but . . . I said her talent was too strong, said Madame. I was right in the wrong way. There is something more than talent here, and she is going to do something for Lion, if he is wise.

It was over in a few minutes. It had gone, but it would come again . . . over and over again if I am not very much mistaken, said Madame. But I wish it could stay as it was then. The last quiver of the last chord, loud and . . . searing, said Madame, there was no other word for it . . . had died away and there was a pause. Then . . . "I think it is beautiful," said Madame gravely. Those five small words meant more to Hilda than anything that would be said to her in her life again. She shone with happiness.

But I was right, thought Madame, she is too dominant for Leda, too strong. . . . At this moment Hilda could dance Leda because, at this moment, she loved Lion and was subservient to love. Now she was in the state of being eager, trembling, pliant . . . as they oll are, thought Madame . . . and, in a curious way, again it pleased her to see that the serious conceited cold little snake Hilda was not exempt. She is ripe for Leda, exactly ripe now, diagnosed Madame, and she wondered how long it could last. I hope it will last the season, she said. It should, not? It is only three weeks, and she thinks it will last for ever. You may lose it in any second, she said silently to Hilda. Any single little thing may spoil it. It's brief, it's brittle. You can break it easily. . . . But in spite of this warning Hilda looked as safe and unconscious as anyone caught up out of the world to a separate pinnacle. But you will have to come down, said Madame jealously.

She tried to turn her thoughts away. "How did you write this? What made you think of it?" she asked Hilda.

"I . . . don't know," said Hilda. "It came to me."

Madame nodded approvingly. She approved of that. "That is rright," she said gravely. "It came to you. You didn't make it up. That is what so many of them say. It came to you, it was *vouchsafed* to you," said Madame severely. Afterwards, when she came to write other ballets, Hilda often thought it was.

"I found the Carlorossi *Fantasia and Variations,*" she said slowly. "They gave me the first idea of it. I thought they fitted. I showed them to Mr. Felix. He thought so too. That is how it began."

Mr. Felix came. He heard, listened, and saw. "And when do you want it?" asked Mr. Felix. *"Tonight?* You want to have it in the programme tonight? My dear Anna!"

"I mean to have it in the programme tonight," Madame corrected him.

"It's quite shorrt," Madame argued. "It only takes a few

minutes. It is really only a divertissement, only you couldn't call it a divertissement, and Hilda has arranged the music down to the last bar."

"Off records," said Mr. Felix dryly. "Then you will use the records? For tonight?"

"I have an orchestra, not?" said Madame. "Why shouldn't I use it?"

"Because, to begin with, there isn't a score of that Carlorossi in London, or if there is, I don't know where to find it."

"You are not trrying, Felix,"

"Anna, there isn't time to try."

"Couldn't you, not, score it from the records?"

"I could, in several days. I thought you wanted it for tonight."

"You are very disagreeable," said Madame.

"But, Anna . . ."

"You are never enthusiast. Never."

"Well, what can I do?" asked Mr. Felix and out of his bright forget-me-not eyes he watched her.

Madame walked away to the end of the room, back again, beating her clenched fist into the palm of her other hand.

"Lion?"

Lion shook his head.

"I tried to get a score as a possibility for Hilda," said Mr. Felix. Hilda looked surprised. "I tried everywhere I know, and I know everywhere."

"The Metropolitan? Great Marlborough Street? B.B.C.?"

"All tried. No one has it."

"But there must have been a score, to make the records. We must go to the makers."

"There wouldn't be time," said Mr. Felix. "It would take all day, perhaps two days, to unearth it, even if they could find it. Still, we might try."

"Miss Parkes, go and ring up. Take the records and see what you can do."

"Could we broadcast for it?" said Hilda.

"We could," said Felix. "If anybody had it it would probably be in Wales or somewhere like that."

"Ilse could go to Wales and fetch it," said Madame.

"Anna . . ."

"You could."

"I could," said Miss Ilse, "but . . ."

"Not in time for tonight," said Mr. Felix. "Still . . . it may not be in Wales. Lion, you will have to go personally, to Broadcasting House."

"That would take me all day," said Lion. "Let's think of something."

"Oll of you think," urged Madame. "Ilse," she accused, "you are thinking of something else. Not of me and this trrouble at oll, not? I know you when your face looks like that . . ."

"Anna," interrupted Miss Ilse. "I was thinking of Madame Rosa."

"Madame Rosa? *Yes!* Madame Rosa! Get on to her, Ilse, im-me-diat-ely."

"Madame Rosa?" asked Mr. Felix.

"She is Spanish," said Madame. "She is the widow of Miguel, the conjuror."

"If she is Spanish, why is she 'Madame'?"

"Because she is clairvoyant."

"I . . . see. Then she will divine for the score?"

"No, of course not," said Madame crossly. "She has every score that is in existence, prractically. It was not Miguel who was the collector. It was his father. His father was head clerk in Pasqual's in Madrid."

"Pasqual's! They had everything," said Mr. Felix.

"Of course. Why do you think we have been talking? Wasting our breath?" said Madame. "He collected scores, and when he was not a Fascist or a Franco or whatever the others were, he brought them to England. He died, and Madame Rosa has kept them. I hope she has kept them. Ilse, you must go to her at once. She lives in Clapham. You know Clapham, Ilse."

"No," said Miss Ilse.

"Zanny will know, but don't send Zanny or she will quarrel. If she doesn't know, the laundry will know, because it was Madame Rosa who told us about the laundry. Get on to the laundry and you will find out. Don't look so bewildered, Ilse. It's not so far to Clapham."

"Not as far as Wales . . . or Milan," said Miss Ilse, with rare spirit.

"Can we telephone her first?" asked the more merciful Hilda.

Madame Rosa's number was found out from the laundry and Miss Ilse telephoned her. Madame Rosa said she would look for the score but it was early and first she must have her coffee.

"Coffee!" cried Madame. "When have I had coffee?"

"Ages ago," said Lion.

"You must be reasonable, Anna."

"If I am reasonable, this ballet won't go on."

Miss Ilse telephoned again in a few minutes and five minutes after that. Madame Rosa then said she refused to look for the score.

"There," said Miss Ilse. "What did I tell you?"

"You must go to her, Ilse. You must explain to her, beg her, plead her. Do anything. Tell her I am sorry. Tell her anything. Don't pull that face to me. Shouldn't I go myself if I could be spared? Go with her, Felix. After oll it is your business. Please, please go. Ah, what a trroublesome woman! How impatient. Won't wait one little minute. I don't understand how people can be impatient like that," said Madame. "Felix, you must get a taxi and go with Ilse. Ah! What else is to happen this morning!"

A minute later Madame Rosa telephoned to say she had after all, on second thoughts, as a favour to Madame Holbein, looked for the score.

"And she has it?"

"She has it."

"Ah! Ilse! Thank God! Tell her a thousand thanks. A thousand thousand thanks. Say I shall send her tickets, say I shall send her a bottle of good brrandy—when I have one. Say . . ."

"Wait," said Mr. Felix.

"Wait? For what? We have the score. What do you need now more?"

"The parts," said Mr. Felix.

"Parrts? What parts? Ah, the orchestra parts!"

"Yes, the orchestra parts. The score is no use without parts."

"Dear God in Heaven!" said Miss Ilse.

"Stop talking, Ilse! Go. Ask her, has she the parts?"

No. Madame Rosa regretted, but she had not. There was silence.

"You could wrrite them," said Madame.

"By tonight."

"Of course. What else? You could, Felix. There are not so many. We could shut you up oll day by yourself . . ."

"Thank you," said Mr. Felix but he did not say no. He said, "If you have a rehearsal of *Noble Life* . . ."

"We won't have a rehearsal, or, if we do, we can manage. Danielli can conduct. We can manage with him. We can manage anything if you will write those parrts, and get it ready in time. The orchestra can be called, for when you wish. Lion and Hilda will stay here to rehearse with you . . ."

"I shall need three copyists," said Mr. Felix. "Pah!" He threw down his pencil. "What is the use of talking, Anna? Where will you get three copyists today? They are all working on films. No, it's impossible I tell you, Anna. Im-poss-i-ble!"

"Lion," said Madame, "go and get me Edmund White on the telephone. Edmund, personally, Lion."

"But . . . shall I get him personally? Won't there be a *battery* of secretaries?"

"Tell them it is Madame Holbein," said Madame grandly, and then her certainty cracked. "Tell them how imporrtant it is, how little time, how urrgent . . ." She stopped herself. "No! Don't tell them any of that. Tell them it is Madame Holbein."

Mr. Felix was dry and refused to become excited, but Madame had not, from the beginning, a moment of doubt that he would do all in his power to help. He had thrown all the cogs he should in her wheels but no others; "It was his duty," said Madame. "They were not cogs, they were knots that had to be untied if he was to do his worrk."

"You make me giddy," said Lion.

The artists were another thing. Noel Streete had no telephone; she sent the unwilling Miss Parkes round to his rooms, but his landlady said he had only just come in and gone to bed and no one dared wake him . . . " 'until he has slept it off,' she said," reported Miss Parkes.

"Ah! Why does everyone conflict me so?" cried Madame. "Very well. We must get Moron. Pierre Moron. I don't like his work so well, but it is better for this than Mathilde's, and he is very fashionable."

"He did the re-dress for *Cimarosiana*," said Hilda.

"It wasn't a success," said Lion.

"A re-dress never is," said Madame sweepingly. "I have told you, Lion. It must be one; choreographer, artist, composer must be parrtners, but for this, this ballet, we shall have to contrrive." She looked at Hilda. "*Now* what is the matter, Hilda?"

"If it isn't to be properly set, I had rather it wasn't done," said Hilda mutinously.

"Who said it shouldn't be properly set?" demanded Madame. "Because I say we shall have to contrrive it doesn't mean that we should compromise, be expedient." Now she could use that word derisively . . . as it is meant to be used, said Madame. "We must use our wits," said Madame, her eyes sparkling. "You don't trust yours. I trrust mine."

Pierre Moron saw the ballet, and was immediately filled with compliments and hope. "It's exquisite, *but* exquisite! And raw. How raw! I like it raw. And that overbearing sexual force that is so rare . . ."

"It isn't rare at oll," said Madame. "It happens oll the time. Now, can you do this, Pierre, do you think? Yes or no?"

"Given time . . ." said Pierre charmingly.

"You know there is no time."

They were in the theatre to give Pierre Moron the proportions of the stage, its height and depth and lighting and fittings. "He ought to know them," said Lion. "As well as *Cimarosiana* he did *Orientales*."

"And just as badly," said Madame. She was beginning to be cross with Pierre. Time was passing every moment and he did nothing but admire and flash his eyes at Hilda. They were fine eyes, black, large, brilliant as diamonds. But too large to be real diamonds, thought Madame. They must be false, and he should leave Hilda alone when I am here, not? It isn't polite to me. "Well, Pierre," she said. "I'm waiting."

"I see it," said Moron, half shutting his eyes.

"What do you see?"

"*Attendez*. I'm telling you. First the Swan. I see the Swan," said Pierre. "A close-fitting all-over costume, like tights, you understand, but all over—arms, head, everything —fitting the whole torso and painted, painted in flaky grey-white, tempera perhaps, to give the idea of coldness, close-fitting over the head, even the hands; non-human, stiff, cold as a shroud," said Pierre. "We could make a mask to cover the face. A mask of mosquito netting, stiffened with plaster of Paris, perhaps, and plaster of Paris feathers on the shoulders and knees."

"How should I dance?" asked Lion. "How should I breathe?"

Pierre considered. "We should leave holes for you to breathe through," he said kindly. "It would be a little stiff, but very effective."

"The Swan must have wings," said Hilda.

"Wings?"

"I don't see him with wings," Pierre objected.

"I do," said Hilda. "He must have wings."

"Leda should be blue," said Pierre.

"Blue all over?" said Madame caustically.

"She is virginal, yes?" Pierre ignored Madame.

"No," said Hilda. "That isn't her quality."

"She is virgin. You say so."

"It still isn't her quality."

"That is how I see her."

"Then you see her wrong."

Lion stared. If Hilda had been Madame she could not have been more crisp.

"Pierre. Come now. Try," said Madame.

Pierre, injured, opened his eyes. "I *am* trying, but if Miss . . . Miss . . . quarrels with me all the time . . . what can I do?"

"You can do nothing," said Madame fiercely. "Nothing at oll. What they are oll talking about in you I don't know. Miss Parkes, take Monsieur Moron away, and Hilda, if you must be so difficult, you will please to hold your tongue. I am giving you this production, not, and how can I if you upset the cart oll the time?"

"The Swan must have wings," said Hilda.

"Lion, you must go for Noel. You must bring him. You must get him awake somehow and you must make him come."

Noel was still in his evening clothes when Lion brought him. He sagged with illness and tiredness; his face was yellow-green and the whites of his eyes were yellow-brown and bloodshot; he looked at the light obliquely as if it hurt him, and he was sullen and apathetic.

"Noel, I have to ask you . . ."

"Damfool to ask me an'thing now, this bloody time a mornin'. Have y' a black handkerchief?" said Noel.

"A black handkerchief?"

"Yes, want it for m' eyes. M' eyes feel bloody wrong."

"They mustn't feel wrong now. I need your eyes," cried Madame in anguish. Then she rallied herself. "Lion, you have a black scarf. Miss Parkes, fetch Mr. Streete a large whisky and soda."

"No soda," said Noel. Madame was glad Miss Ilse was gone with Mr. Felix to Madame Rosa.

When the whisky came, she guided Noel into a seat, touching him with the tips of her fingers. "Now, Miss Parkes, go and tell Zanny to make a large pot of strong black coffee, hot, verry hot, and bring it back here." She let Noel sit still, let the whisky soak into him before she signalled to Lion.

She did not explain anything. She said, "Look." He should understand that no matter how bad he is, thought Madame.

She had been afraid that the music would hurt Noel's head, but he seemed unmoved by it. He sat by her, his hands hanging loose, his head pushed forward at the stage, his eyelids, that were puffy and red, heavy over his eyes. He smells sodden, thought Madame. His whole body is sodden. And to think of the things that are shut up in that body.

Poor Noel. She was angry with him too. He isn't pitiful, he is wicked, she said.

Once he spoke. "What is it?"

"Leda and the Swan."

"Hmmph!"

When it was over he said, "Who did it?"

"The girl. Hilda French."

"Hmmph! You want me to do it for you?"

"Yes, Noel."

"For when?"

Madame took a breath, looked at his face and away again, and said, "For tonight," and waited for his explosion.

But Noel only nodded and said, "I thought so. When you sent for me at this damfool hour of th' morning."

Madame waited.

"I would do it for you, if I could," said Noel.

"You *could*, Noel."

"M' dear, with what? I'm not a bloody conjuror. I can't make a set or dresses out of th' air."

"We can improvise."

"Like a damfool village pageant?"

"No! No! Not at oll," said Madame, in a flash of temper. "Would I ask you? Use your sense, Noel, if you have any left. No. Firrst decide what you want, and then we shall rransack London," said Madame, "the whole of London to find it."

"It takes time to ransack-hic London," said Noel and gave a sudden yawn. "London-is-so-big."

"Noel, you are not to go to sleep. Miss Parkes, where is that coffee? Give Mr. Streete some coffee and then tell Hilda to come here."

Hilda too was tired with a bad night, continual dancing, much emotion, and no breakfast. She did not like the look of Noel. "Why did you bring him? He is drunk," she said, offended, like a little puritan, to Lion.

"He is always drunk," said Lion, as if that were an explanation.

"Then why does Madame let . . ."

"Wait," said Lion. "You will see," and as Hilda looked still unconvinced he said, "You didn't like the Moron, did you?"

"No."

"Noel Streete did the sets for *The Other Island*," said Lion, "and *Collage*."

"Did he?" Hilda's eyes opened. "Is he *that* Noel?"

"That Noel," said Lion. "Wait. Leave him to Madame."

When Hilda came near Noel part of her was offended by his looks and his smell, part of her was interested and instinctively respectful of something she recognized as alive in this sodden heap of a man. It is that Noel, she thought. But how dreadful he looks.

He stood up when Madame introduced him, holding on to the seat in front of him with one hand. "It was clever of you to write that," he said. His voice was husky and bleared, but he looked at her intently from under his weary lids. "How old are you?"

"Seventeen," said Hilda.

"Seventeen. Lucky," said Noel. "Lucky. Don't you go and tie yourself up now with any bloody nonsense. You keep yourself clear and one day . . . one day, hic . . ." He held the back of the seat more tightly and turned away from Hilda. Presently he turned back again and asked, "How do you want it dressed?"

"I want the Swan to have wings," said Hilda immediately.

"How can he dance in wings?" said Madame.

"He can," insisted Hilda.

"What about his lifts?"

"They must be swinging wings," said Hilda. "Not stiffly fixed, fixed so that they can swing."

"I see what you mean," said Noel, brooding. "I . . . see . . . what . . . you mean. Great wings and feathered, like Icarus."

"Even bigger," said Hilda.

"Even bigger," said Noel. "And? What else?"

Hilda, who usually had so many ideas that she could hardly choose among them, hesitated. "Anything I think of seems banal," she said. "Feathers . . . tights . . . they all give the idea of an imitation, an unreal swan. I . . . haven't been able to think what else he should wear."

"Because he shouldn't wear anything else," said Noel. "He is savage and wild." Her eyes closed to think of that, and then widened, bright with interest. "Isn't he?" said Noel.

"Yes. Yes, he is."

"Except for the wings," said Noel, "he should be naked."

"But he can't be naked . . . on the stage, Noel," said Madame. "Not on my stage."

"It doesn't matter what damfool stage," said Noel irritably. "He must be whitened, his whole skin. He can wear a G-string," he said irritably to Madame, "feathered, with the feathers just fitting the hipbones. And, like a savage wears, feathers round his wrists. Yes, he must be whitened, his face and his hair . . ."

"A white wig?" said Madame doubtfully.

"A wig won't do. No damfool wig," said Noel violently. "It must be his own hair, whitened with something that thickens it and mats it and makes it stiff, so that it suggests a casque of feathers, but stiff, not soft. Ordinary wet-white whitening should do; if that isn't stiff enough, whitewash. It must be done some time before so that it sets."

"Oh, well, I dance nothing before it," said Lion, "and I can have a bath after, I suppose, in time to dress for *Noble Life*."

"I will do you myself, Lion," said Noel.

"You watch while Joe does it," said Lion prudently. "Go on."

"The webs," said Noel. "Those webs are important. They are a horrifying part of a swan, big, powerful, black. We should paint your legs black to the thighs . . ."

"Paint? Why not tights?"

"The texture," said Noel briefly. "They must be skin,

swarthy and matt, but if we do that it will foreshorten you, make you thick-set. No, we shall have to go without it. You must have black shoes and your eyes must be made up to look heavy, painted with that stuff Indians put on their eyes, kohl, and you must have a red spot on your forehead between the brows. We must try it now. There isn't time for maquettes," and he said to Madame as if she were Miss Parkes, "Get wet-white and whitening. Better get white-wash ready as well, in case, and grease-paint, let's see, black and a blue and vermilion, I think, and the trunks, not trunks but a covering, and the feathers . . ."

"Zanny and Miss Porteus can take those off the *Swan Lake* dresses, Miss Parkes. Tell them."

"Yes, Madame."

"And the wings. You must get great white towering wings," said Noel, "almost as high as Lion himself."

Madame, Lion, Hilda, Miss Parkes, looked at one another in silence. "Get wings!"

"But, Noel . . ."

"You said you would get me whatever I wanted," said Noel. "Now you can."

"But, Noel. Can you think . . ."

"How can I think if you go on talking to me? How can I work your bloody thing out? Come here," he said, jerking his head to Hilda, "Listen."

"Call Miss Porteus and Zanny," said Madame. "Lion, would the Metropolitan . . ."

"I can ask them," said Lion doubtfully, "but I don't think so . . ."

"They had wings on the dreamboat in the last act of *Swan Lake*," said Miss Parkes.

"Those were wooden," said Madame witheringly.

"Even paper wouldn't do," said Lion. "It would rustle."

Miss Ilse came in, spent and white, but with a look of secret elation that Madame knew. Like a cat that has been at the cream, said Madame. She has been in, over the way. She turned her back on Miss Ilse. "Zanny. Miss Porteus," she said. "We have to make Lion a pair of wings."

"What is he?" asked Zanny. "A fairy or an aeroplane or a beetle?"

"Zanny, don't be rude to Madame," said Miss Ilse.

"I'm not rude to Madame."

"Ilse, don't interfere. You don't know what we are talking about. You are too *late* to know what we are talking about. You didn't come in with Felix, not? I know where you have been."

"Anna . . ."

"Wings take days, Madame," said Miss Porteus.

"These can't take days. We must have them this morning."

"That isn't possible, Madame."

"It must be possible. It can be possible if you choose."

"Anna."

"Be quiet, Ilse. Anything can be possible, Miss Porteus,

if you have enough will. That is what you haven't . . . enough will. You have no courage, Miss Porteus, and that isn't what I like to see in you . . ."

"Anna . . ."

"Ilse, *will* you not interrupt. I say we must get those wings today and we shall get those wings."

"You had better ask Miss Ilse to work a miracle for you," suggested Zanny tartly.

"I can," said Miss Ilse. "Anna, I have been trying to tell you. The Convent has wings. They have most beautiful great feathered wings, shaped right to the ground from the shoulders; all made of long white feathers, on stiffened frames. They use them for the Archangel Gabriel and for angels in the tableaux. They move most beautifully when they walk; the nuns will lend them," said Miss Ilse. "I knew Hilda wanted them, so I went in on my way to ask."

Hilda and Noel were talking of Leda. "She will have to have her dress torn off her," said Noel.

"*Not* on my stage," said Madame again.

"It's difficult to find a suitable dress for that," said Noel moodily, as if he had not heard her.

"There is a picture . . ." said Hilda hesitantly. She was respectfully hesitant with Noel. "You . . . you know it, of course. *The Nativity* of Piero della Francesca in the National Gallery. Do you remember the dresses of the choir of angels?"

"We seem full of angels, not?" said Madame, and she said sharply, "What are they like?"

"They . . . could tear off," said Hilda, "leaving only the underdress. There—there would be a contrast between the high-necked looped gown and the underdress, limp and soft. I think . . . dark deep red, a brown-red for the over-dress, and . . ."

"Scarlet underneath. The colour you are wearing," said Noel, his eyes looking down on Hilda in the sequined scarf. "I'm not sure of the shape of the gown. Let's take a taxi to the Gallery and see."

Madame opposed this. She did not want to let Noel out of her sight. She did not want Hilda to go with Noel. "No," she said. "You two needn't go. Hilda mustn't get tired."

"If she wants to have her *décor* done she must get tired," said Noel. "She has to work."

"But you needn't go to the Gallery. I can send Miss Parkes for a copy of the picture. Miss Parkes or anyone." She had a feeling of danger, an antenna that told her that if Hilda went with Noel it would, in some way, destroy her mood for Lion. . . . Why? I don't know. How? *Look* at Noel and then look at Lion. How could it? I don't know, said Madame, but it could.

"Miss Parkes, or whatever her name is, can't bring the colours," argued Noel. "We shan't be long."

"But, Noel . . ."

"Madame, I must. . . ."

"I can't spare Hilda."

"I must have her."

"No, Noel."

"Yes."

Madame was nearly exhausted. Olways . . . when you have things arranged, this, this character crrops up. "Noel, my dearr!" she began, and, discarding her exhaustion, she put her hand under his arm and turned him towards her and began to talk to him.

"Oh, very well," said Noel after a moment or two, and flung away from her. "I suppose we needn't go."

"For colours, no," said Madame. "You have them oll here in your head; and to see Hilda, no. Hilda has other things to do, and so have you, Noel."

"You are a slave-driver," said Noel, but he did not say it crossly. "I must go home for my things."

"I shall send for them," said Madame quickly. No, it would not do for Noel to get away; she might not see him again. "You can work here, Noel. You have to work here, not?"

"Have you a back-cloth without dye on it?" asked Noel. "Get it put down; and what colour curtains have you? I shall need them to mask in the sides."

"They are grey," said Madame. "Grey-grreen."

"Good," said Noel thoughtfully. "Yes, good. Couldn't be better. Get someone to ring Elibanks. They can probably send two of their boys or a girl along. Tell them to bring two buckets, mixed grey-green, and brushes and a stipple brush."

"I don't want it stippled, Noel."

"Not stippled, to finish it off evenly," said Noel. He was

looking at the stage, measuring it with his eyes that were so nearly closed that Madame was afraid he was going to sleep again standing up.

You not only have to light the fires, she said irritably to herself, you have to keep them burrning. She called Miss Parkes and told her to give Noel another cup of coffee. "See that it is hot firrst," she said; she suspected that Miss Parkes was capable of lukewarm coffee.

She was grateful that she had neither jerked Noel nor spoken to him when he looked up. "Was it the *Gossip Review*," he asked, "that showed those French postcards in a cut cloth of paper lace?"

"Postcards? In paper lace?"

"Yes, it was small, quite small." His eyes measured the proscenium again. "I believe it would do . . . if we can get it. If they have still got it. Lion," he called. "Here, Lion. Come here."

"But . . . Noel . . . you are not going to put Leda into a frame of paper lace?"

"Wait," said Noel abstractedly. "Wait. Lion, is Glancy here? Good. Now listen. You must get on to the Gossip, the Gossip Theatre, and ask for Munro Jennings and ask him . . ." he walked away with Lion. ". . . might fit here . . . no time to make it." He was showing Lion what he meant, measuring with his hands; now he did not look shambling, nor as ill, and his voice was clear. "I think he is going to do it," said Madame to Hilda, who was standing near her. "I think he is going to be oll right."

Hilda left Madame and went to them. Glancy joined them. They stood in a group talking, oblivious. Then Edwin, the young electrician, came on the stage. Lion called him down. "Good," said Madame. "They should begin to think of lights." She watched them with growing content. "It's going forward, not?" she said.

Lion went away to telephone and presently came back. "Yes, they have it, but it's torn, and one of the battens is split."

"I can get on to that," said Glancy. "We can patch it."

Miss Porteus came down with a tape measure and measured Lion as he stood talking. She had the velvet heart pinned to her dress; Madame could see the pins gleaming in it as she knelt to pass the tape round Lion's thighs. Madame could hear her sniff as she paused and wrote the measurement down on her little piece of paper. Poor Miss Porteus, thought Madame. I mustn't forget Lollie at four.

"Zanny thinks it a pity to spoil the *Swan Lake* dresses," said Rebecca. "I am going down to Wardour Street, to get some feathers."

"Has anyone gone to the Gallery for Noel's picture?"

"Yes. Alma came in. I sent her."

"And Felix? How is Felix doing?"

"He has shut himself in the classroom. Miss Ilse has put a table for him there. She has taken him some breakfast."

"The copyists should be on their way from Broadwood," said Madame.

"Mr. Felix needs more manuscript paper. Shall I get it?" said Miss Parkes.

"Yes. And who should go to the printers? Miss Parkes, you should go there at once though it won't be any good. Send one of the girls for the paper."

Glancy came up to them. "Please, ma'am. Mr. Streete says can we arrange for a lorry to go to the Gossip."

From a lorry to feathers. What a mixture of things can go to the making of a ballet.

Now Lion went to the gramophone. "Where are the records?"

"Mr. Felix has them," called Hilda.

"Get them from him, Miss Parkes. Say he must give them up for a little while. We shall brring them straight back. Lion and Hilda have to rehearse to show Edwin for the lights."

As they danced, a back-cloth came down and Madame saw Noel with a boy, and a girl in an overall, her hair tied in a handkerchief, come on the stage with buckets and a step-ladder. Behind the dancers she saw Noel explaining to them; he had a sketch on a piece of brown cardboard. He and the girl conferred, went to the buckets, and stirred up the paint. Noel tried it with a brush. Then they began to lay it on in the same grey-green colour as the curtains. Neither boy nor girl paid the slightest attention to the dancers, and Hilda and Lion modified their steps so as not to crash into the buckets.

"Now they are oll working in together, not?" said Madame with growing satisfaction. I tell you," she said to Miss Ilse, who had come up behind her. "It is worrth oll the pains when you see it grrowing like this. Slowly, slowly grrowing."

"It isn't slow. It's marvellously quick," said Miss Ilse. "I don't know how you have done it, Anna. It's miraculously quick."

"It isn't quick enough," said Madame, her eyes brooding. "I feel anxious about those copyists for Felix."

"They have come," said Miss Ilse, "and I have brought you an egg flip."

"Ah, Ilse, I hate them!"

"It has brandy in it," said Miss Ilse. "I have one too for Hilda. The child must be exhausted."

"Did you put brandy in hers?"

"Yes," said Miss Ilse firmly.

"Madame." It was Noel. "I want something for feathers, drifting down. At the beginning, before the Swan comes, when Leda is alone, gathering shells. Something for a drifting feather, or feathers. The Swan's feathers drifting down. Torn tissue paper looks like snow."

"Real feathers?"

"No. Either too insignificant or too heavy."

"Anna . . ."

"Wait, Ilse. I am trying to *think!*"

"But, Anna . . ."

"*Ilse!*"

"What is it?" asked Noel, turning to Miss Ilse.

"I'm trying to tell her," said Miss Ilse, flushed, "I used to cut paper feathers when I was a child. They wouldn't look like snow because they are shaped. Cut paper feathers would be the right weight," said Miss Ilse.

"They would," said Noel. "They would." He smiled at Miss Ilse, and Miss Ilse smiled back at him. That is currious, said Madame. I had thought Ilse would be shocked at him and she isn't, not at oll, and I have never seen Noel smile at anyone before.

"Here," said Noel. He was holding in front of her the cardboard sketch she had seen him showing to the two young painters. "I have had to do everything roughly," said Noel. "Couldn't make anything but sketches for the dresses, and I roughed out this."

Now she saw what he meant to do with the frame. It was narrow, of white feathers framing the stage . . . feathers? I suppose they are feathers, but they might be white coral or seaweed, but anyhow white. The back-cloth was grey-green, stormy, "We shall make it look more stormy and then change it with the lights," said Noel, but its grey-green was stormy already, deep with a tinge of greengage. "The curtains are the right colour, or as near as," said Noel. "Just as well, I have enough to do with those bloody feathers."

Then they are feathers, thought Madame.

"Well, is it right?" asked Noel.

"I think it's extrremely clever," said Madame. "I don't know how you thought of it. It seems to me, now I have seen it, exactly right . . . which is queer," said Madame, "because I never could have seen it for myself."

"Blue shells . . ." Noel was saying to himself. "Blue shells . . ."

Miss Porteus and Zanny came back about Hilda's dress. The picture had come and from it Noel had sketched a rough design. "We can get the dark red, more maroon it is, from one of the mantles from *Collage*," said Zanny, "but for the scarlet underdress . . . there is only that scarlet gauze sari of yours, the Benares sari, Madame."

"You wouldn't cut *that*," said Miss Ilse, glaring at Zanny. "That lovely thing!"

"What else then?" said Zanny. "Perhaps you have time to go all round London looking for it, and you can look till you drop and you won't find that colour, and it has to be *made*," said Zanny.

"Ah, don't quarrel me oll morning, I can't bear it," said Madame. "Is there time to quibble over this and that, I ask you, Ilse? Cut it, Zanny."

She and Miss Ilse stood and watched Hilda and Lion working together on the stage.

"Anna . . ."

"Yes, Ilse."

"Anna, it's not . . . indecent, is it Anna?"

"It's not indecent," said Madame.

"N-no," said Miss Ilse. "The dress *would* tear, with a swan," said Miss Ilse judiciously. "I always think swans are terrifying, but . . . it's very strong, Anna," she said faintly.

"It's strong," said Madame. "This isn't a children's matinee, Ilse. It is for adults, not?"

"I hope it's not too strong," said Miss Ilse.

Mr. Felix had come in. "I shall have to get the harpist back. I need a harp."

"Well, get him then."

"If he will come. He worked six rehearsals without a performance, and now we want him to work a performance without a rehearsal. But perhaps he will come."

"Felix . . ."

"Anna?"

"Felix, Ilse thinks the Swan obscene."

"Anna, I *didn't* say so."

"I can see it by your face. Felix, will it offend their taste? The English taste?"

"It wasn't invented to please it," said Mr. Felix, watching the stage.

"But . . ."

"As that is neither here nor there, I think it will," said Mr. Felix.

"Offend it or please it?"

"Please it."

"There now, Ilse."

"He didn't say it wasn't indecent," said Miss Ilse. She paused. "And, Anna, who is to pay for all this?"

"It won't cost much, hardly anything, Ilse."

"Hardly anything can be a great deal. Noel paid fifty pounds for that framework from the Gossip Theatre. I heard Lion agree to it on the telephone."

"Ah, Ilse, let's do it firrst and count it later."

"But, Anna . . ."

Madame steeled herself. Sometimes it took all her nerves to disregard Miss Ilse.

"Oll my life, whatever I wanted to do, Ilse, you have said 'Don't.' 'Don't.' 'Don't, Anna.' 'Be careful.' 'Don't do it.' 'Don't take a risk.' If I listened to you I should be sitting at home knitting and reading Sunday books. Go away from me. You are a raven, croaking and croaking and croaking. Isn't it oll going perrfectly well? Why do you throw your doubts on it then? It couldn't be better, Ilse."

Miss Ilse was not listening. "Anna," she said, "Caroline is here."

"Caroline?"

"Yes. She is watching Lion and Hilda," said Miss Ilse. "I don't think she is pleased."

Madame had gone to her sitting-room. "I need a few minutes, Ilse. I must think what this oll is, I must reckon it. If anyone wants me I shall be in my room. They can come to me there, and see Miss Parkes about the printers. They must get it through for us, Ilse . . . and don't let Noel go away." She said that as a parting injunction.

She went up to the sitting-room and sat down at her desk and rested her head on her hands. Now she had time to think of it, her head was spinning. Reckon it! I can't, said Madame. How can one ever? How can anyone tell the cost of doing any little thing? But jubilance filled her. I can't reckon it, but I have done it, she said. I don't know how far it has come, but it has come a considerable way.

She was sitting at her desk that, every day, Miss Ilse arranged tidily and that, in the first five minutes Madame spent at it, she made untidy again. On it were lists, block sheets of designs, letters, a wire basket of bills. These began the day on Miss Parkes' or Miss Ilse's desks but were gradually transferred to Madame's, where there was great difficulty in finding them again. "Madame, please, have you seen Driscoll's bill?" "No, why should I?" "But . . ." "I have never had it, never!" declared Madame, but Miss Parkes found it in her desk. "Anna, that answer to General Cook Yarborough . . ." "What answer?" "I put it on your desk for you to sign." "I never saw it. Wait, I have signed it, not? Where is it? It isn't here. It must be somewhere." Miss Ilse found it pinned to the back of a design, and Madame had drawn a blue-pencil sketch on it.

There was a heterogeneous collection of things among the papers: an illuminated card that Miss Ilse had laid there for her to see; some pressed primulas in a sheet of old yellowed tissue paper that had been sent to her that morning by an admiral who alleged she had thrown them to him in his box from her bouquet years before in Panama. But why primulas? thought Madame. They would be so difficult to throw? And I don't think they have primulas in Panama?

There was an edition of the child's book, *Peter Rabbit,* in French, and there was an oblong red case of which the velvet was worn.

Madame sat idly turning over the pages of *Peter Rabbit.* She had bought it for Lollie.

"Why should dancing be in French?" said Lollie. "Why should we have to learn all these names in French?"

"Because it is the language of dancing, as Latin is the language of the Catholic Church and medicine and plants."

"But why not plain English?"

"You are an English pupil," said Madame, "but in the same class with you is Calliope, who is Greek, and Lao-Erh, who is half Chinese, and Lippi's little brother, who is Italian. Why should they worrk in English?"

"Why should they work in French?"

"Ballet is international, and it must have a language that can be understood by oll. By trradition its language is French and its tradition has been handed down, even to you, Lollie—and to Calliope and Lao-Erh and Archie and Giacomo and Zoë and Miette. I am glad you have asked me. Even the smallest dancer should understand the dignity and history and tradition of her art."

Holding the little book, Madame thought of Lollie and Lollie's class, her "eggs." If she shut her eyes she could hear the scattering sound, between a slither and a scamper, they made as they ran across the floor in their light shoes when she called "Places."

She saw the feet, standing all alike, the arms lifted in

unison showing the small armpits that, in the little girls, had a pearly allure that was far older than they; chins were turned dutifully over shoulders, leg muscles strained and swelled in their efforts to please, thighs turned out, each calf, each instep, was held rigid, the toes pointed in black or white or pink shoes laced over socks. They were held, rigid, then moved all together, to the right, to the left, to the right, arms changed, heads turned, all alike, all adroit.

I know them oll, said Madame, not only their bodies, but their charracters, their sulks and smiles, their pluck and . . . no pluck, said Madame. I can read them, their foreheads and legs and minds and hearts. I am not often wrrong, thought Madame. I was even right in a way about Hilda. I kept her in spite of my feeling against her. I had enough judgment for that. I must not forrget Lollie's audition, thought Madame, and she read in the book: *Il fut attrapé et mis en pâté par Madame McGregor.* . . . Poor Lollie, thought Madame, and smiled.

She laid down the book and picked up the red velvet case and held it for a long while in her hand. She pressed the catch slowly, lingeringly, and as the lid came up she saw the old diamonds sparkle from the dark rubies and she smiled. You have hearrd me speak of this, often . . . the words formed themselves in her head. It was given to Marli the great Italian ballerina when she came to St. Petersburg from Milan as guest artiste for a single performance of *Giselle.* It was given to her by the Tsar, with his own hand, when she was presented. She gave it to me when I came back to the Moscow Festival as a guest artiste myself. I had been her pupil while I was in Italy, I went to Milan to study with her, and she was in Moscow when I came there to dance. I had meant to keep it olways, till my death, but I see that I should allow it to go on. Now you have come back to me, as a guest artiste in my little theatre in your little way. It is only a little way, of course, but, because I believe that you are to do great things, I am giving it to you. I want you to have it, Caroline.

She saw Caroline, her head with its plaited bronze hair, the eyes, the curved face, the white neck, soft shoulders, lovely arms; she saw her in the parts she had had . . . so far, said Madame. "Prelude" in *Sylphides*. The golden "Valse" in *Nutcracker*. One of Prince Florestan's sisters in *Aurora's Wedding*. Chosen Virgin in *Sacre du Printemps*. She is coming, thought Madame. Coming fast. She touched the cross with her finger. But you didn't choose to dance for me last night.

She found herself advancing reasons and excuses: she who never allowed excuses. Caroline had been working oll day. Rehearsals and the performance. She was tired. A bad rehearsal makes a good performance . . . but it was Lion who said *that* tarrydiddle, said Madame, and she shut the box with a click. I shall see how you dance, she said, and then she opened it again. No, she said. One must have faith, not? I shall wrap it up and put it on her table in her dressing-room. I *know* she will dance well for me tonight.

There was a knock at the door. It opened. It was Caroline.

"I am sorry to disturb you, Madame."

Madame looked at her with love and indulgence. "You don't disturb me. You give me rrest, dear child. Come in and shut the door. You may sit down."

Caroline did not sit down. She stood opposite Madame, her hands holding the back of the chair. Her face was angry; there was a red patch on each cheek and her knuckles showed white as she held the chair.

"What is it, Caroline?"

"You didn't mean me to come here this morning, did you?"

Madame stared amazed.

"What are you talking of, dear child?"

"You didn't mean me to know anything about this until tonight, till it was too late to change."

The love and indulgence left Madame's face. "It is too late to change," she said evenly.

"I shan't accept that," said Caroline.

"What do you mean?"

"I refuse." Madame did not answer. "I can refuse," said Caroline. "I am not under contract here."

"Certainly you are not under contract," said Madame. "I put none of my dancers under contract. They are free to go whenever they think they must. I don't keep them."

"Madame . . ." Caroline's gaze flickered and fell as it

had when she would not face Madame from the stage. "Madame, I can't be treated like this."

"How are you treated? Pre-cise-ly as before."

"That isn't true."

"I don't tell lies, Caroline."

"I came here as prima ballerina . . ."

"Ballerina? What are you thinking of, Caroline? You are far too young, too inexperrienced to . . . to have that honour," said Madame. "Do you know what a ballerina is? You should think before you say, dearr child! We have no ballerinas here. You are our guest. You have gone further, a little further, than the others, so I give you the biggest parrt, the principal role, tonight. My favorrite part. A bigger role than any you have had so far. Then what do you mean?"

"It . . . it's out of all proportion," said Caroline, indignation in her eyes. "First you let Hilda put on *Lyre,* and I could have told you it wouldn't be a success, and now this . . ."

"You have seen the new ballet, then?"

"Yes."

"You thought it was promising . . . ?"

"It's beautiful," said Caroline. "It's one of the most beautiful things I have ever seen."

"You didn't object to *Lyre* because you didn't think it would be a success. You object to this because you think it will. Then am I rright, Caroline, in saying you are jealous of Hilda?"

"Of *course* not."

"Then?"

"She didn't dance herself in *Lyre*, but this . . . It will take everything," said Caroline slowly. "You know it will. It will take the whole programme."

"I hope it will take its place in the programme," said Madame. "We needed it, Caroline."

"You can't put a young untried dancer beside me."

"Not if she puts herself there?"

"It's such an indignity. She is no one."

"Everyone was no one once. I didn't think, in making room for Hilda, I was hurting you," said Madame. "I didn't think you could be hurt by Hilda."

"But—think of who she is and who I am."

"If she is who you say she is, no one, a young untried dancer, how can she hurt you? If she isn't, she is in her rrightful place. Then why are you afraid?"

"I'm *not* afraid." That stung Caroline.

Why is it, how is it, thought Madame, that I should be driven to taking the part of that little serpent Hilda against you, my Caroline? She looked with infinite misery at Caroline. Caroline did not look full of beauty now, she looked fearful and angry . . . and stupid, thought Madame suddenly. Yes . . . and soft. Things have been too easy for you olways, thought Madame. You have had them too much your own way. She thought of that meadow, that panoramic meadow that she had never seen. Caroline is like a meadow, Hilda is like the road . . . that I came on, the hard highway. But who was Hilda to expose Caroline to Madame, to show her these things she did not want to know? She isn't only a serpent, said Madame. I was rright. She is Eve too. Eve with her fruit of knowledge.

"Caroline," said Madame, and her voice was very gentle. "You have gone so high. Are you not going higher? Not?"

"Of . . . of course I am," Caroline stammered. "I hope I am."

"I wonder if you are," said Madame. "I wonder if you are."

"That isn't fair," cried Caroline. "Just because I defend myself. You know we all have to fight, fight hard for our places. If we don't push ourselves, who will? Very well, I am jealous of Hilda. I have to be. All dancers have to be. Hard and jealous. When you were my age I expect you were often jealous yourself."

"I certainly was not," said Madame. "I was far too prroud."

"You kept your position."

"Of courrse I kept it, but not by being hard to other peo-ple—by being hard on myself. Of course I kept it. No one could take it from me. You should watch that for yourself, Caroline. Perhaps you are right to feel yourself in danger. I tell you, Hilda gave the better performance of the Lady last night. She danced it with her whole body and soul, you danced it with the tip of your little finger."

They faced one another across the desk. Madame felt she was turning to stone. She had been trembling but now she was not trembling, she was cold with a numbness that was creeping up from her feet, up her legs and thighs to her heart.

"I have to be trruthful about these things, Caroline."

"Very well. I shall go," said Caroline. "Then you may have Hilda. Hilda, body and soul, for the Lady. But you have forgotten one thing," she said, and she looked at Madame with triumph in her eyes. "If I go . . . Lion will go too." She saw the instant stricken look on Madame's face, and said with spite, "He came here as my partner. He will go with me."

"Lion came here as my pupil, firrst," said Madame. "He is still my pupil, learrning with me."

"Only out of hours," said Caroline. "Only as a hobby," said Caroline tauntingly. "If I go, he will go too."

"You belong to a Trade Union, then?"

"No, of course not, but he is my partner, not Hilda's. I chose him."

"The Metropolitan lets you choose your partners, not?" said Madame caustically.

"I am not talking of the Metropolitan, but of something else. Something I was looking forward to telling you," said Caroline, with a look of the old Caroline in her eyes.

"What is it, Caroline?"

"I have a chance to get into the Ballets Internationales—with Leonid Gustave."

"With Gustave?" Madame's voice could not help warming. "Ah, Caroline! That is what I have olways wanted for you. Olways. There is only one Gustave. There will never be another. Ah, Caroline! I am *delighted*."

Caroline did not warm or waver. "Lion wants to go with me," said Caroline gently and spitefully. "There is a chance he might, but, of course, if he stays here without me, I shouldn't dance with him any more."

"I see," said Madame.

"You can't blame Lion. He is only thinking . . ."

"That you are more use to him than I," said Madame. She sprang up, knocking her chair backwards, and hit the desk top with her open hand. *Pierre Lapin* was knocked into the waste-paper basket, the red case on to the floor. "Did Lion think you could come here and say these things for him? No, he must say them himself. Fetch him. Fetch him here in front of me."

Lion came. He stood in front of her desk in his dark-blue sweater and tights, and the sun fell on his face and on his broad shoulders and curled dark hair, but his face was sullen and his eyes would not look at Madame, nor at Caroline.

"Lion, is this true? Do you do this to me?"

Lion smiled. "Don't smile," said Madame sharply.

"Do you, Lion?"

Lion looked up angrily as if he were caught and trapped in this nest of women. "Can't we arrange something?" he said. "Perhaps Hilda would be content if you gave her her production with Caroline in the part. She should be. After all, Leda doesn't matter very much, it is the Swan . . . I want to dance the Swan. I want to dance it," said Lion to Caroline, who made not the slightest response. "Or why shouldn't you double the part, Hilda one night, Caroline the next? You have the Lady," pleaded Lion. Caroline still did not answer.

"There has been enough of this discussion," said Madame. She had to hold to the desk and the coldness was on her neck, in her head, in her lips, so that she could hardly make them speak. "I cannot be told, and not told, what I am to do with my own theatre. By you, you *children!*"

"We are not children."

"Children, that you should trreat me as if I didn't know, as if I were . . . *inutile;* that you should think so little of the thing you do, you would destroy it wantonly. Where is the discipline, the rrespect?" cried Madame. She might have cried, Where is the love? She said, "You have nothing at your hearts but your little cold self-interest." She saw the red case on the floor at her feet and, clumsily and stiffly, because she was so cold, she bent down and picked it up. She stood, looking at it.

Where is the love? she might have said. The discussion is ended. She did not say that either. She said, as she had said at the end of each class that they, either of them, had ever had with her: "Very well, you may go."

"Madame . . ." began Lion.

She never heard what he had to say. The desk and the lists, the red case in her hand, Caroline, Lion, the room, were suddenly swung sideways. A dizzying cold whiteness came up from her knees and hummed in her ears. But colour hasn't a sound, she said, and then she heard Caroline cry out and knew that she was falling.

"Lion!" cried Madame, "Lion." She felt his arms come round her and catch her as she fell.

Chapter Six

IT WAS Miss Ilse's arm, cold, bony, faithful, that was under her head when she woke. Not woke, opened my eyes, came to . . . to oll this care and trrouble. Opened my eyes to what I must see. "But need I see it, need I?" whispered Madame.

Miss Ilse's arm was faithful but comfortless; those others had been comforting but faithless. What can comfort me now? thought Madame. She turned her face away from all of them and it was, surprisingly, her pillow that she turned it into, her pillow cool against her aching eyes. She had not seen her pillow for a long while . . . "a long long time," she whispered. Miss Ilse was putting a shawl round her, her soft Indian shawl that was large and deeply red . . . "red as roses," whispered Madame. It mitigated the coldness, like sitting near a fire, and the pillow was cool and white as snow. Fire rose red, snow white, white and red olways for me. She was still cold, but the numbness had gone, she was able to shiver, even her teeth were shivering. But teeth don't shiver, they ch-chatter, thought Madame. But **no**, mine are shivering silently.

Someone came and put hot-water bottles at her feet and sides. From the brown hands, smelling of soap and a little of onion, from the firm wide tread so different from Miss Ilse's flutterings, she knew it was Zanny.

"*T' n' sens pas bien d' tout,*" said Zanny, smoothing Madame's hair. "*Petite reine. Mignonne.* Zanny will take care of you."

"I can take care of Madame, thank you, Zanny."

"It appears not," said Zanny.

"You know how headstrong she is . . ."

"Never with me," lied Zanny. Miss Ilse knew she lied, but her fright and worry made her absurdly vulnerable. "There! You see, that is all you can do. Weep and pray. Pray and weep," chanted Zanny. "I . . . I am making in the kitchen a good strrong soup. She will drink that and gain her strength."

"She doesn't like soup."

"Not your soup. She likes mine. A soup with little *croutes* . . ."

"Go away, the both of you," said Madame. "I am not a bone for you to fight over. You make my head worrse. Go away. Take your soup and prayers away. Leave me alone."

"You must try to sleep, Anna."

"How can I sleep? When everything . . . when . . . when . . . the printing is not arranged for, and now it will have to be altered. When Felix's copyists . . . And the wings," cried Madame. "And what about that lorry, Ilse? Has Miss Parkes come back? And Rebecca? Noel wanted us to ring Eli . . . Eli . . . those scene-painter people. . . . Edwin. It's time they thought about lights . . ."

"Hush. Hush," said Miss Ilse. "All that is arranged. It's all arranged . . . at least it was arranged," she said sadly.

"I must get up," said Madame.

"Not yet, Anna. At least for an hour. I have never known you to faint before. I must get a doctor."

"I don't need a doctor. I need to deal with this." She struggled to a sitting position, the shawl fell away and a hot-bottle slumped to the floor, but the humming whirling whiteness came round her again. "I can't . . . get up," said Madame.

"No, no, Anna! You mustn't. Tell us what to do, and we shall do it."

"I don't know what to do," said Madame. She said it flatly and lay back on the pillow and closed her eyes. Shades were closing down on her. She saw, under her lids, the vast shape of Zanny pulling down the blind, and moving out of her line of vision, away. Madame made one more effort. "Tell . . . tell . . ."

"Yes?" said Miss Ilse.

Madame shook her head on the pillow and motioned Miss Ilse to go away.

Chapter Seven

ZANNY'S hand had drawn the blind so that the room was wiped out in darkness. Madame was left in a pool of quiet where there was no noise, no cold, only the grateful cool and warmth and quiet. She tried to grip her senses . . . my five wits, said Madame, but she was sliding into sleep. She needed sleep as if it were healing and she slept, not deeply but lightly, and in her sleep she was extraordinarily clear.

Niura, that is a nightingale. It was so quiet that she could hear it now. The streams of music, raucous impolite disturbing music, were wiped away under it; the demanding, querulous voices had ceased to hammer into her brain. The quiet had wiped them out, and in the quiet she could hear the nightingale. Her eyes were shut; their eyes—Miss Ilse's anxious and easily swimming in tears, Mr. Felix's boring like two little blue weevils, Hilda's hidden by her lids, Lion's bright . . . but not meaning a worrd they say . . . Caroline's fine blue ones that looked only inwards at herself, Noel's with their discoloured yellow-brown bloodshot whites, Moron's false and black, Lollie's young leveret ones —could not look at her now. She could hear the nightingale beyond the birch trees and it was sweet . . . sweet, and, in the garden before dawn, not in Russian woods but in the London dew, birds were singing. *To hold your hands is like holding two birds in my hand. Anna, my darling. Anna.*

"No," said Madame, and she said it aloud in her sleep. "No. Don't disturb me now. Ah no! Let me rest. Rrest."

Rest was not long, any more than love, for her. She was restless. Now she was the Humming-Bird, dancing instead of Archie, as Archie, that night. She was small and she was breaking in her own small shoe in the hot theatre wings. She saw the pan of rosin, her toes were firm, padded, in the shoe, and she worked it and felt the stiffness leaving it. She bent to lace the ribbons; she felt the unaccustomed pull of her tights at the back as she bent forward and the coloured ends of the feathered wings swung from her arms; she was breaking in her shoe and the shoes were under the glass dome like two soiled pink sugar mice. Now she was grown and it was long gauze skirts that fell away from her as she moved, gauze skirts and grave-eyed marguerites, and now she had a little gilt trumpet, and round rouged spots on her cheek; the Queen's hand in the white glove was held out for her to kiss, and the black tutu of Odile tilted round her as she curtsied. Perhaps I am going to die, said Madame. Perhaps at last they have killed me. She felt sorry for herself. I have never fainted before, and, in the last few minutes before you die, the past comes back to you, not? But that happens oll the time, said Madame. Time passes, but that is what it doesn't do. Past, present, and future. Her past and her present, her future if she were not going to die, were all dancing. Dancing-dancing-dancing-dancing-the dance-the dance-the dance—that was like the clocks ticking. They had begun to tick in . . . Berne? was it, or Dresden? (She did not know which clock it was in here) . . . and had gone on ticking ever since as the labels had been pasted on to the baskets and the foreign letters came. I could paper the walls of my sitting-room with the stamps on the letters I have had from abroad this year. Oll over the world. They are pedigree dancers. She fell into another uneasy sleep in which she had Marli's cross, the diamond cross, in her hand, and there was no one to whom she could give it, no breast to which she could pin it. "But it isn't a medal," cried Madame in her sleep; but, in her hand, it had become one. All over the world. Madrid, Milan, Cairo, Chicago, and Calcutta, Johannesburg . . . *The moon is my country.* Who had said that? Pierrot, and Pierrot is the no one in us all, that lonely no one who is left alone at last. No one. No-one-no-one-no-one, ticked the clock and, deeply, tired out, Madame slept.

She was woken by Hilda asking, "Is it good?"

"Why should it be good?" she answered exasperated. "How do I know what it is? I haven't seen it."

She did not know which answer she had given, but she was wide awake. The coldness and whiteness had gone, she could sit up, on her elbow, and see the darkened room. The clock was ticking still, very clearly. Something-for-something-something-for-something, said the clock.

"Ah no!" cried Madame aloud, and lay down again.

It would be Hilda to wake her, even though it were only the thought of her. Hilda, the serpent, Eve with her fruit. "Go away," said Madame. "Go away," but Hilda was saying what the clock had said: "Something for something," said Hilda.

Madame's head ached, and her bones. Her eyes felt as if they had not slept, but the sound of the clock, the thought of Hilda, had come between her and her pillow and presently she lifted herself and sat up again and thought, What is the time?

The room was too dark for her to see. Giddy, and beginning to be cold again, she put back the shawl and swung her feet on to the floor. The electric fire was on and its glow lay in a circle on the carpet; she stood in its warmth and shivered. Then in her stockinged feet, giddy and weak, she walked uncertainly, with this new clumsiness, over to the window and pulled up the blind. The light made pain leap in her head and dazzled her eyes but she stood there until she grew used to it. She turned to look at the clock. It was five minutes to four.

Something is to happen at four, said Madame. But what? What?

Where is Ilse? she thought. Why isn't she here? She never is here when I want her. You would think she didn't understand what had happened. And *what* is to happen?

asked Madame. She called, "Ilse. Ilse," but there was no
answering flutter and rustle. She does nothing at oll, said
Madame. Nothing at oll to help me.

She knew that everything was yet to happen, but she
could not grasp it. Her mind, no less than her body, felt
weak. She was still in the borders of her faint and her sleep
and the confusion of her distress. She was old, old and un-
resilient. Distress and worry surged back in her. Why didn't
I die? she said. I thought I was going to, then why didn't I?
It would have saved so much trouble. With honour, they
would have cancelled the perrformance tonight.

She put her hands to her head that ached so that the
temples throbbed and hurt as she touched them. What will
happen? What can I do? Lion . . . But there was no Lion.
No Lion, and Caroline had gone, walked out of her life
. . . because I will never consent to see her again. Never.
But what can I do? She could not think. Thought led into
a labyrinthian tangle of all they were doing and not doing:
Felix, feathers, harpist, lorry, copyists, lights, Noel, whitening, the Benares sari, Miguel the conjuror, lights . . . I
must alter the programme, thought Madame, Ilse must get
Driscolls . . . but what is to go in the programme? And
who? . . . Who?

She looked down from the window and saw that it was
raining; quick rain was driving between her and the road.
She felt for her shoes and put them on and went through
into the sitting-room. From its windows she could see the
theatre, but the rain cut it off; the wistaria looked heavy

and sodden, she could see no lights, hear no sound. She stood by the window looking out into the rain, and the clock in this room sounded clearly too, loudly ticking. Something-for-something! ticked in her head.

"If only I could think," she whispered. "If I could find one thing, clear, that I must do. I could start with that. It would lead me in again. Something, however small and unnoticed. It would do to start with, something clear and simple, by itself. What could I do? Speak to Noel? But what is the good if . . . See Lion's wings? But he isn't to wear them. . . . Ah! If I could only think." Her thoughts would not go forward. They went irresistibly back to bed, with the pillow and the shawl and the warmth and quiet when she could sleep and dream and hear the nightingale. Then, into confusion came one small clear thought, by itself. Lollie was the freshet. "Of course," said Madame aloud. "Lollie's audition at four. I promised her I should be there."

A promise is a promise, it is a prrinciple, said Madame. You can *not* go back to bed, she told herself. You will now go down and keep your promise and take Lollie into the theatre to Edmund White. When it's most difficult to keep a promise, that is the time you should, that is its *proof,* said Madame. That I shall go down and keep my prromise to Lollie and then I shall see what I shall do.

She went to the mirror that hung over the fireplace and looked at herself. Better not to look, said Madame quickly, and, without going in to her bedroom to tidy herself, "Not even as much as to pass a comb through your hair!" as

Miss Ilse said to her afterwards, she went downstairs. She had caught a glimpse of an old white wrinkled face with dark patches under the eyes and massed untidy hair. I expect I look like a witch, she said. A witch without a potion or a brroomstick to ride away on. I wish I could rride away! Never mind. A promise is a promise, she said, and I have to keep it. I can thank Edmund for the copyists even if they came to no purpose. And after . . . She could not think about after. She ceased to think and went on her way down the stairs.

There was no one in the hall, but, on the chest, two men's hats were lying, a broad white scarf, a stick, and a pair of gloves. Now where have I seen that scarf, that stick, and those gloves before? She picked them up; the scarf was of heavy silk, the stick was malacca with a silver band, and the gloves were fine. Evidently a someone, thought Madame. I know them. Then they can't be Edmund's. I don't know Edmund's stick and scarf and gloves, but I know these. Whose can they be? She looked at the two hats. Someone else has come with Edmund. Someone I know. They have come and Ilse has taken them over to the theatre. I must go.

She went through the classroom, and there was the table Miss Ilse had put for Mr. Felix. Sheets of music were strewn on it, his ink bottle, blue pencil, pencils, were there, but Mr. Felix had gone. I expect he went home, thought Madame. It was no good his staying, not?

As she passed the window she saw that the theatre lights

were on. They glittered through the rain. Madame did not let people see her weep; "I only crry on the stage," she said, but now she was alone, and when she saw those lights a sob suddenly shook her. Be quiet! Madame said to herself. How can you go and meet Edmund, if you do that? She spoke so sternly that the sob was choked down. She opened the door to the back staircase and met Miss Ilse face to face.

"Oh, Anna!"

"Oh Anna!" mocked Madame. She was suddenly furious. "I could have died up there by myself. Where were you? Where have you been?"

"Anna . . ."

"Answer me. Where have you been oll this time? Letting me sleep as if there were nothing to be done." She looked at Miss Ilse with suspicion. "You have been over to the Church."

"Only for a moment, Anna . . ."

"I am ill!" said Madame bitterly. "And you leave me alone. Ill, beaten down, in trouble, and you go to church. To church! Zanny is quite rright!"

"When we are in trouble," said Miss Ilse with dignity, "naturally I go to church."

"Naturally," mocked Madame.

"Yes, naturally," said Miss Ilse. "I went to light a candle to St. Jude. That seemed to me the best thing to be done. The *best!*" She looked back firmly at Madame. "You see, I believe," said Miss Ilse. "But, Anna, what am I thinking of? I came to tell you . . ."

"Tell me nothing," said Madame rudely. "Keep away from me. Don't speak to me at oll," and she brushed past Miss Ilse and went down the stairs.

Lollie was waiting in the big girls' dressing-room and with every minute she grew more afraid. "What do you do when you are thoroughly frightened?" she had asked Miss Ilse as she came through on her way upstairs.

"Say a Hail Mary, that always helps me," said Miss Ilse kindly as she passed.

Lollie did not know how to say a Hail Mary. She did not know what a Hail Mary was. That was no help to her.

Auntie was no better. Miss Porteus had found time to come from the theatre to "look the child over" as she explained to Zanny. That was exactly what she did do. She looked Lollie over and over despairingly. "Your tunic is too short," she said with her unhappy sniff. "You look all legs. I don't know how you grow so much." She tightened Lollie's bows that were already too tight, but Lollie said nothing, because Auntie had bought the ribbon for those bows. "Real silk ribbon, not rag," said Lollie. "Well, I hope you get it," said Auntie. "But I don't suppose you will. You have never been what I should call a taking child, at all. Seems to me for the cinema they would want curls. You never had the vestige of a curl. Blue eyes are what they like and dimples, and you are downright skinny," said Auntie. "Still, you never know. You may get it. Unlikely things *do* happen. We could do with it with my arthritis. I'm crippled today, crippled! Well," said Auntie with another sniff, "don't let's meet our troubles till we get them."

"No, Auntie."

It seemed to Lollie they had several troubles now. Food, for instance. She was hungry. She thought of what of all the things in the world she would like best to eat, if you could get all the things in the world. "A banana sundae," thought Lollie.

"We are not very hungry, are we?" Auntie would say. "Let's put the kettle on and have a nice cup of tea and some bread and butter, or a bun or a pie from the little shop round the corner, or a kipper." "A dancer must dance on her stomach," Madame said, which made the others giggle. It did not make Lollie giggle. She understood it; she understood it sharply. She had such difficulty to dance on hers.

She heard that in Lion's company, the Metropolitan, the corps de ballet started on five pounds a week.

"Five pounds?" said Lollie. "A *week?*"

"Yes, how little!"

"How—how *much!*" said Lollie.

"You are too young to understand how little it is," said Madame.

Lollie was silent because she was certain that Madame did not understand how much it was. She knew that Madame did not understand, as she and Auntie did, how to spend a pound . . . or a shilling, or a penny. "The price of a cup of tea." People often said that, but how many of them knew how much it was? Five pounds, thought Lollie. Auntie and I could live on that. I could buy four hundred kippers and one thousand two hundred cups of tea. I could buy fifteen pairs of shoes in one week! Why, I could keep Auntie and she could have arthritis in peace!

As soon as Auntie left her, she took off the tunic that was too short. Lollie did not know much, but she knew it was not wise to look leggy at auditions if it could be avoided. "It pays to dress." That was another of the things that people said. How did one pay? They did not explain that, but there was a way round every difficulty, Madame said. Lollie knew of only one way round hers, and that was to do about the tunic as she had done about the shoes and take someone else's. She stepped over to Zoë's shelf. She chose Zoë because Zoë was the best-dressed child in the school. Yes, Zoë had left her tunic. She shook out Zoë's nicely folded tunic and tried it against herself, looking in the old long mirror that had been relegated here from the class-room. Its fly-brown marks came across her face, but she could see that she looked considerably improved in it. The tunic was rose-coloured, which made her look less pale; it was full and gathered, with far more material than her own, which made her look less skinny; and, given a tunic of the proper length, she did not look leggy at all. Lollie put it on, folded her own away, and sat down on the table to wait till she was fetched.

It isn't stealing, said Lollie, it's only borrowing, and I shall be found out, because Archie may be in the theatre, and if he is, he will tell. Oh, well! said Lollie, and she might have added, Beggars can't be choosers.

To think about money was better than a Hail Mary, whatever that was. Money was the most familiar, the most sobering thing Lollie knew. She decided that, till the moment she had to dance, she would say her money tables.

Four farthings, one penny,
Twelve pennies, one shilling,
One thousand and two hundred cups of tea, five pounds.

She looked up and saw Madame.

"But . . . Miss Ilse said you couldn't come."

"Ilse is a fool," said Madame. "I promised you, not? You must learn, Lollie, that people keep their promises."

Lollie was silent. That had not been her experience, but, certainly, Madame had come. She looked at Madame. Madame looked odd; her clothes were puckered as if they needed what Auntie called "a good pull-down"; her stockings were wrinkled, and her hair looked like a thatch and her skin looked tired and . . . pouched, thought Lollie. "*Are* you better?" she asked doubtfully.

Madame said she was, but, when she held out her hand to Lollie and said "Come," her hand was colder than Lollie's own. Why should my hands be cold when I am so burning hot?

"They have arrived," said Madame. "We must not keep them waiting."

"N-no," said Lollie and understood that, in Madame's

eyes, even the victim was obliged to have good manners. But
. . . I don't want to go into the theatre. The time has come
and I don't want the time to come. I can't do it! cried Lollie,
by Madame's side, without a word.

I don't want to go into the theatre, thought Madame. The
moment I do it will start oll over again . . . it will do
that because it must, and I am not equal to it, said Madame,
but together, hand in hand, she and Lollie walked silently
across the garden to the theatre door.

In the garden Madame took a deep breath. The rain fell
against her face, quick and soft; it chilled her but it was
freshening, and she stopped and lifted her face and saw the
width of the sky, between trees and roofs, filled with rain
clouds; a rift in the cloud showed a vision of light and grey;
the light struck the rooftops and a weathercock on a steeple;
the wet slates shone and the gold cock glittered; there was a
smell of wet soot and earth and grass, and from the wistaria
bunches a wave of scent came out to her, warm and wet
with the fresh rain. I pinned my faith to that wistaria,
thought Madame. I was a fool. You shouldn't pin your
faith to things, or people . . . but you have to, said Madame. If you are to live at oll you have no choice.

As she opened the door, a gust of music swept past them
into the garden, welling out from the theatre, which was
ablaze with lights.

She could see Mr. Felix's head as he conducted. The
light shone on his skull under his white hair, and she could
see his hand, in its white glove, lifted as he held his baton.

The Carlorossi theme welled past them, overfilling the theatre. "It's too big for here," said Madame aloud. "I was afraid it would not be; orchestrated, it might have been blatant, thin; but it isn't, it is big."

Above the orchestra, on the stage, the curtains were pulled back and Noel's set was there; the frame with its painted white curling feathers set in gold, and the stormy grey-green background lit so that it looked threatening and deep. "But . . . it is perrfect," said Madame.

As she looked, the first white swan-feather floated down and Hilda was on the stage. *Leda, looking for shells on the lake shore.* Madame watched her walk on, always a critical moment to Madame, but she saw that Hilda had it easily in her grasp; she watched, nodding approval as, in the contained little looped maroon gown that, swinging open, showed a sudden line of scarlet, Hilda passed into the opening of her *adage*. Madame did not know how long the passage lasted; she watched enthralled, nodding her head; occasionally she smiled.

Then the music changed to that loud downbearing whirring rush, and Madame suddenly gripped Lollie's shoulder so that Lollie cried out. Lollie, staring, saw an immense white Swan, towering with its wings, with swept-back feathered hair and black-marked eyes; Madame saw that the Swan was Lion.

Lion! "But . . ." said Madame. "But . . ."

Lollie twitched her sleeve.

"Wait, Lollie."

"But, Madame . . ."

"Wait."

"Madame . . . are those them?"

" 'They,' Lollie . . . 'Are those they?' "

"Yes, but are they? Which of them is him?"

" 'He,' Lollie. Who?" Madame reluctantly tore her eyes away from the stage and followed Lollie's gaze, to where two men stood between the stalls talking, with Miss Parkes and Rebecca standing respectfully by. She saw first the one she had expected to see, the flat pink face, grey hair, and monocle of Edmund White.

She looked past him to the other, a little square man with a Mongolian forehead and skin and eyes and small gesticulating hands. She gave a cry, and Lollie quickly moved her shoulder out of reach. "It's Gustave!" cried Madame. "Gustave! Gustave himself!" Now who, thought Madame swiftly, who has Gustave come to see?

Chapter Eight

HILDA had not heard the quarrel between Lion and Caroline. She did not know there had been a quarrel. When Lion had leaped off the stage she had waited for him to come back. She did not understand that he had left her with the ballet half-rehearsed, without warning and without apology. Perhaps Hilda was conceited. It had not occurred to her that Lion could do that.

"Where is Lion?" she said presently to Rebecca. "I'm waiting for him."

"I don't know," said Rebecca helplessly. "Caroline was here, very angry with him and with you."

"With me? Why?"

"She is jealous."

"*Caroline*, jealous of *me*? Don't be absurd, Rebecca."

"Well, she has gone storming off to Madame, and Lion has run after her."

Lion has run after her. The impact of what that meant hit Hilda between the eyes. "Lion, run after Caroline when he . . . when I . . ." and Rebecca saw Hilda blush as she had not known that Hilda could blush, a deep burning painful red.

A kiss can be a very big, or a very little thing. It depends on who you are, thought Hilda. She had let Lion kiss her and she had kissed him and now it seemed to her that, as Madame said she overdanced, as she had overdone herself in *Lyre,* she had given too much away to Lion, been generously reckless or recklessly generous. She blushed now and burned to think how strong she had been, and this was not from modesty but from pride. When am I ever going to learn? thought Hilda despairingly. I hate myself. I hate . . . hate Lion.

However she tried to belittle him, he stayed as Lion. Even as she said she hated him, she felt again the way he lifted her, the way he turned her towards him and let her slip down, her body against his, held firmly and, she could have sworn, loved, in his arms. She felt the warmth and smooth health of his skin, the way his eyes looked into hers, teasing and commanding; Hilda had never been teased or commanded by a man before. She remembered how angry and hurt she had been against him in Madame's office yesterday . . . was it only yesterday? . . . and how, as soon as he touched her, she had melted. But that is purely physical, she said austerely, but was it? Would she have liked Lion to touch her, hold her, kiss her, if she had not loved him? She knew she would not. But . . . it's ignominious to love where you are not loved. He . . . he is a Golden-Syrup

Lion. She argued and burned with shame, and still he still was Lion.

But there is a difference, thought Hilda proudly. Nothing I do now will be done willingly. Before, I gave in completely. I capitulated. He has killed that. If ever I give in, it will be with reservations. She saw those reservations as high impenetrable fences that no Lion on earth could hope to scale or look over. She hoped they would stand firm.

"Caroline says she will refuse to dance tonight," said Rebecca.

"Let her." Hilda, naturally, did not mind that in the least. "I can dance the Lady," she said.

"Without Lion?"

"Without *Lion?* Rebecca, you don't mean . . ."

"Caroline says if she goes, Lion will go too."

"But, she couldn't do that. She hasn't the power," said Hilda.

"Caroline has influence and money," said Rebecca. "She has always had Lion under her thumb, and we all know what Lion is."

Except me, thought Hilda bitterly. What a fool I have been . . . but her private troubles were drowned under this greater implication.

"She . . . he . . . they couldn't do that to Madame, now, at the last minute. It's unspeakable. It would be dastardly."

"What words you use, Hilda. It would be dastardly, but

they could do it. You don't know yet how mean dancers can be, a great many of them, mean and petty and jealous. Here comes Miss Ilse with the news," said Rebecca, and she said seriously, "It *is* that news, Hilda. She is crying."

"God help us, what shall we do?" wept Miss Ilse. "Anna. Anna. It's the first time I have ever known her to take off her hand for a single moment. Now she . . . she . . . God forgive them!" cried Miss Ilse. "I can't. He went after Caroline without a word."

"The times, the times I have had him in my kitchen and given him a good hot meal," hissed Zanny. "We fed him and taught him and kept him. I wish I had thrown it in his face before I saw him," said Zanny. For once she and Miss Ilse were in complete accord.

"Anna . . . oh, Anna!"

"Madame! Madame!"

"Madame, *ma pauvre, pauvre Madame!*"

"Anna! Anna!"

They reminded Hilda of a Greek chorus. She began to be irritated and that took away some of her dismay. Rebecca was not much better. Rebecca and Miss Parkes were busy calculating the consequences.

"Will they be *allowed* to do this?" Rebecca was saying. "Will the Metropolitan countenance it? To Madame? Madame is someone, after all."

"It will be interesting to see whose part they take."

"Will they back their own dancers or Madame?"

"But . . . Rebecca . . . it won't be a public quarrel?" asked Miss Ilse in a quavering voice.

"Won't it!" said Rebecca. "Of course it will," she said with relish.

Miss Ilse dissolved into tears again. "Such a thing has never happened to us, never."

"It needn't be public unless we tell everybody," said Hilda suddenly and crisply. "The Metropolitan wouldn't want it public either. We can say that Lion and Caroline have been taken ill."

"*Both* of them? That isn't likely. Who would believe that? You will never hide it," said Rebecca and Miss Parkes together. They are like two ghouls, thought Hilda, and she said aloud, "Well, if it can't be hidden, we must win."

"Win, with the performance tonight? How can we? Oh, Anna . . . Anna," cried Miss Ilse, breaking into still fresh tears. "What shall we do with the performance tonight?"

"Give it," said Hilda.

"But . . . how can we do that?"

"We must do that. There is nothing else at all that we can do. You must call an immediate rehearsal," she said to Rebecca.

"I? But I have nothing to do with the theatre and the ballets."

"That doesn't matter. It's the authority that matters. You have authority. I will tell you what to do. If I do it myself there will be quarrels and objections."

"She is right," said Miss Ilse, her tears drying.

"But . . ." said Rebecca to Hilda, "can you take upon yourself, in Madame's absence . . . ?"

"Yes," said Hilda, quite certainly. She saw them stare at her and she said, "What would Madame do? Give in?" she asked Miss Ilse. "Recriminate?" she asked Zanny. "Make a scandal?" she asked Miss Parkes and Rebecca. "She wouldn't do any of those things. She wouldn't waste her time. We shall have to rehearse *Noble Life* and *Leda*. Francis must do the Nobleman. After all, he has been the Attendant all this time, he ought to know it. Lippi can take the Attendant, or Hugh."

"And the Swan . . . ? Who for the Swan?"

Hilda stopped. Her thought had stopped too. To think of anyone else as the Swan was unbearable to her. She had written it for Lion, built it on him, built it round him.

"John?"

"No, John wouldn't do," she said slowly. "He is too slight, John would be wrong. Quite wrong."

"Could Francis do it too?" asked Rebecca doubtfully.

"You can have a plump Nobleman but you can't have a plump Swan," said Hilda seriously. "It must be Lippi," she said suddenly, "and Hugh must be the Attendant."

"Lippi? But he isn't up to the others."

"I know, but he is the most like Lion." That slipped out when she had not meant it to, but Rebecca only nodded. "Miss Parkes and I will get on to the telephones," she said. "I shall get Lippi first, he has the most to learn."

"But Lippi?" Madame said afterwards. "You chose Lippi? He is more like a boisterous young eagle than a swan."

"Whom would you have chosen?" asked Hilda.

Madame had to admit that she would have chosen Lippi.

As Rebecca went to telephone, Hilda suddenly called her back. It was an impulse she could not name. "Rebecca," she said. "Don't tell Lippi it's to dance Lion's part, nor Francis. Tell them it's to understudy."

"Why?" asked Rebecca.

"Because . . ."

"He won't come back, Hilda," said Rebecca gently. Hilda glared. She resented that gentleness.

"Lion" . . . "Lion" . . . "Lion" . . . Hilda heard his name in whispers, in derision, in complaint, in anger. "Lion."

"Ah, forget Lion," she cried impatiently.

No one had a good word to say for him. In spite of all she had hoped it had leaked out that he, "and Caroline," Hilda reminded them fairly, had walked out on Madame. "And no one has ever done that before," they said in awe. "She has walked out on us. Never one of us on her."

"I should hope you would have more sense," said Rebecca.

"But to think that Lion . . ."

"*And* Caroline," said Hilda firmly.

"But Caroline isn't as bad as Lion." That was the general verdict, and it was true. Caroline was high-handed, but at least she had acted for herself. "Lion is a follower," said witty John, and Hilda winced. "Not a lion but a jackal," said John.

"Must we play animal grab?" asked Hilda.

"Rebecca said I was to understudy Lion," said Lippi, when they were resting in the wings, she panting and tired, Lippi fresh and eager. "Lion isn't coming back, is he?"

"We don't know," said Hilda slowly. "We are doing this in case he doesn't."

"Madame wouldn't take him back."

"We don't know what Madame will do. It isn't for us to judge," said Hilda primly.

"But he won't," said Lippi.

Hilda was too tired to argue. She had been dancing since early morning in a rising crisis of emotion, and now nothing seemed left in her but the ability to dance; all anger, all feeling of mortification, had left her, but she had an inescapable yearning for Lion. To dance Leda to Lippi's Swan after Lion's was like dancing with nothing at all. Lippi's rushes were like the rushes of the young eagle with which Madame after compared him; he was not tall enough, nor strong enough, nor big enough. She felt tired out, and tired of heart as well as in body and mind.

She left Lippi and went and stood near Noel. Noel was no comfort but, curiously, when she was with Noel, Lion faded a little, into what she felt was probably his proper place. But was it? Were they all wrong about Lion, even she?

"He won't come back, m' dear. I know Lion."

"Don't you ever leave room for anyone to grow?" snapped Hilda.

"Doesn't happen," said Noel, and stood up and stretched his arms. "That's finished." He was not talking of Hilda and Lion but of his cut cloth of feathers.

Ironically, now that Hilda's whole reason for it was no longer there, the ballet was complete. Elibank's young painters were cleaning their brushes; Noel had finished the painting of the last spine and curl of the last feather. "For Jesus' sake don't touch it. It's still wet." The members of the orchestra had come in long ago and had sat smoking and waiting; now Mr. Felix appeared and called them sharply and began distributing the parts. "The ink is dry on them," he said, "but only just."

Hilda went down to him. "Shall we rehearse with you now, straightaway?"

"Why do you think we are here?" asked Mr. Felix, who was in no amiable mood.

"You know Lion has gone. We are managing," said Hilda, not without pride. "Lippi is dancing the Swan."

"Manage with whom you choose," said Mr. Felix. "It's nothing to do with me. I'm here for the music, and the music is the same. I attend to my business. You attend to yours." Though he was grumpy, Hilda had the feeling that he thought she was attending to it well.

When he started to conduct his arrangement of the Carlo-rossi music, pride and excitement welled up in her. He has done it beautifully, beautifully, but without Lion . . . Ah, what a waste! cried Hilda. Lion! How *could* you do that to me?

She had been called upstairs to try on her dress and had kept it on to dance in so that Noel could watch it. Noel turned her this way and that, lowered the bodice, cutting it down between her breasts, lifting the underskirt as impersonally as if she were a dummy. "That will do," said Noel, "or I think it will. Can't tell till I have seen it from the front. Come in front and see it," he told Miss Porteus. The task of whitening Lippi had still to come. "But before I do that," said Noel, "let him put on the wings and trunks and come on the stage with Hilda. Better dance it. I can't see what those wings will do until he dances in them."

"But don't stop Mr. Felix," Hilda warned Noel as he went. "We can come in with him. You don't need to see it all through. Let Noel get down in front," she told Lippi. "He wants to see how the wings look as you come on." She listened. The ballet was nearing its end. "It's just before the climax. We can pick it up there. Where I go on and you come after me, and take me in the big lift." Lippi nodded obediently. He was obedient . . . and that is the last thing the Swan should be, thought Hilda in despair. This was where Lion . . .

In all the times she had danced Leda, Hilda had still not lost the terror of this swoop of Lion's when he came down on her from behind and bore her up, higher than his shoulder; the power of his grasp left her almost paralyzed.

Lippi could lift adequately, gracefully, but no more than that. "Well," sighed Hilda. "It will have to do.

"Now," she called over her shoulder to Lippi. She had her back to him as she danced.

She had not danced this with the orchestra before; after the gramophone it was new, loud, strong, and hotly alive. It made her dance as if she were new too with fresh life. Ah, if only . . . cried Hilda, but she had to curb that and wonder if Lippi were coming, if he had timed it or would be late; then she was swept off her feet from behind with such a force that she cried out realistically with fear and surprise. She was held high, brought violently down and crushed in Lion's arms, against his breast and shoulder, as he carried her off.

"You have been busy, haven't you?" said Lion as he put her down. He was furious. "Who the hell put Lippi in my part?"

"I did," said Hilda icily, but she was shaking with surprise and joy. "He did it very well," she added.

"Lippi!" said Lion. "You little busy-body!"

"Lippi is at least reliable," said Hilda.

"Shut up!" said Lion. "On again," and he turned her round to the stage.

Chapter Nine

"GUSTAVE!" Lollie did not recognize Madame's voice, flattered and shy. "Leonid!"

"Anna! Dear Anna!" He kissed her hand . . . as if she is a queen, thought Lollie.

"Gustave, now tell me, what has brought you here? What have you heard? Whom have you come to see?"

"Whom? Why, you, Anna. Who else, today? It is today, not?"

"Of course, it is my anniversary," said Madame slowly. "I . . . I had forgotten it. *Forgotten* it. It is today." She felt excitement beginning in her in every vein.

"I have come to pay my respects to you, as they say, Anna. My profound respect. Fifty years, and good years, Anna. I think oll London should be here tonight; the part that counts to us will be, not?"

He says *not* and *oll* like Madame, thought Lollie. He is like Madame. They began to speak in French. Always French, thought Lollie . . . and of course far more quickly than she could follow. As she talked Madame's fingers absently smoothed the hairs on Lollie's neck, between the dragged plaits, but her eyes were looking over Lollie's head to the stage.

Gustave was watching the stage as well.

"That is a very remarkable little girl you have here, my dear Anna. How old is she? And it is her work?" He watched again. "She should have a chance Anna, not?"

Madame, with a pang, answered, "Yes." Noel had painted Lion, made up his eyes, whitened his hair. Gustave did not say anything about Lion in the full panoply of the Swan.

These words fell into the air over Lollie's head and reached her ears. She looked at the gentleman, Gustave, with startled eyes. How did he know she was a remarkable little girl when he had not seen her dance?

When the ballet was ended he said, "Anna. I should like to see that again."

Will he want to see me twice? thought Lollie. Fancy having to do it twice. I didn't know Lion and Hilda were having an audition too.

They began again, and, as suddenly as he had asked for it, Gustave stopped it. He has no manners, thought Lollie. "No, I have seen enough," he said. "I shall come again to-night. Tell me about what time. I want to see this again. I con-grat-u-late you, Anna. I told you, Edmund. I told you, she has olways something up her sleeve." He turned. "Well, we must go until tonight. Then I shall want to meet your little dancer. I think you will let me have her, not? And we shall do her ballet perhaps. The young man too. They are good! I mean it. Well, we must go. Good-bye."

"But . . ." said the other gentleman, Edmund. "I must see my child."

"What child? Where? For what? What child? I have an appointment at five."

"I came here to see a child, for *Starlight*. Why do you think I came all this way, Gustave?"

"Well, Anna, give him what he wants. He wants a child. Anna always has plenty. I'm sure she will give you one. Here," he said, catching Lollie by the shoulders. "This one will do. Here is a complete little child all ready."

> *Four sixpences, one florin,*
> *Five sixpences, half a crown,*
> *Twenty sixpences . . .*

"This is the child, Edmund," said Madame, laughing. How could she laugh? thought Lollie. She thought the gentleman Gustave went far too fast. Who was he to give orders?

"Say 'thank you' and bring her along," said Gustave. "We can put her in the pocket of the car."

"Wait, Gustave," said Madame. "This is important for Edmund and for the child . . . Lollie, this is Mr. Edmund White. Say how do you do."

Lollie stiffly held out her hand. Mr. Edmund White looked down on her doubtfully; she looked up, dazed, at him.

"You are very small," he said.

"Yes," said Lollie in a whisper, and then she rallied herself. "There are plenty smaller than me."

"Than 'I,' Lollie."

He bent down and looked at her closely, holding her hand. "Can I see you smile?"

"Yes," said Lollie, not smiling. She had come prepared to dance, not to smile.

"Smile," he said. It was a command, so definite that Lollie recognized it. She smiled her two-edged smile obediently and immediately.

"Does she smile like that always?" he asked. "Smile again." Lollie smiled.

"She smiles with her eyes," said Edmund White. "That is ve-ry satisfactory. Send her up on the stage."

"Of course," said Madame. "Lollie."

It had come. Lollie felt she had no legs, that she was all forehead and eyes and beating heart but, mysteriously, she was up on the stage. *Forty sixpences, one pound.*

"Don't look at the lights."

"No," said Lollie. She saw Mr. Felix ready for her, and took her stance for the opening of the variation.

"No, not to dance," said Edmund White. "Walk over to the left and look back at me and imagine you are asking for something." That was easy. She imagined she was asking for a banana sundae.

"Superb," said Gustave. "What more do you want, Eddie?"

"Smile again." Lollie smiled. He smiled too.

"But . . . can she dance?"

"Oll Anna's children can dance. Do you think she would have shown her to you else? Anna knows much more than we do about dancing? You can leave that to her."

"I like her," said Edmund White to Madame. "I should like to have her along for a test. I should like George to see her. I love that smile—woe-begone, wonderful! I like her. . . ."

Lollie waited patiently, nerved to dance. Her moment, even if it were a lean little moment, was here. She was ready. *Eight half-crowns, one pound.* She stood ready, her arms ready to lift, her foot in the first *dégagé,* her ear cocked to Mr. Felix, her eyes and her smile waiting for Madame's nod.

"Good-bye."

"Good-bye, Anna. Good-bye."

"Till this evening. You are coming, Eddie?"

"Good-bye."

Mr. White came down to the orchestra rail. "Good-bye Lollie. I shall see you soon. You smiled very nicely."

Lion and Hilda stepped out of the wings. Mr. Felix had stood up and turned round to bow. Madame and Miss Ilse, followed by Rebecca and Miss Parkes, were walking up with them to the entrance. Everyone had turned their backs. Daylight shone in for a moment as the outer door was opened and shut. They were gone.

"They . . . he . . . he hasn't seen me dance!" said Lollie.

No one heard her. Lion and Hilda, full of excitement, had run down to the dressing-rooms. Mr. Felix was arranging his music, and the men were climbing out of the orchestra pit one by one; the flautist emptied his flute into his saucer and put it away and went out wiping his mouth on the back of his hand as if he were thirsty.

Now Glancy and another man in stained blue jeans came on to the stage, pulling on ropes so that the frame slowly lifted up and Lollie saw the weights coming down. The grey-green back-drop was drawn up and the yellow one with the square tower and poinsettias came down for the *Cat Among the Pigeons.* She could see Glancy turning the great iron handle and the ropes moving. The other man brought on the Nun's seat. "Out of the way, Christmas," he said.

"You can't put that here. I have to dance," said Lollie with dignity.

"No more dancing until tonight," said Glancy.

"But . . . they are coming back. They must be."

"Not they. Off to their tea. Seen all they wanted to. They won't come back."

It was true. Emile and Zanny and Mrs. Pilgrim the charwoman from the house had come in and were sweeping between the seats and up the aisles. They wouldn't be sweeping if anyone important . . .

A woman in a dark dress and two girls in green overalls

came and began carrying in boxes and tubs of flowers, flowers such as Lollie had only seen in shops; they were all the same—white and red carnations, green ferns, and white jessamine. The air had been full of the dust from the brooms; now it was heavy with scent. Even in her hurt and dismay Lollie breathed it in with reverent admiration. What it must have cost! thought Lollie. In her life, Lollie would have many flowers herself, bouquets and baskets, but she would never lose that instinctive feeling about them. What it must have cost.

"Please, dear," said the woman in the dark dress, coming across the stage and pushing Lollie out of her way. Then Miss Parkes came on with her notebook and pencil. "What are you doing here, Lollie?" she asked. "Run away and change."

"Lion and Hilda danced twice, twice!" said Lollie in a trembling voice. No one answered her.

"The carnations *grouped*," the woman was saying to Miss Parkes, "and the jessamine, like spray, along the edge."

The heads bent over the ropes, over the brooms, over the notebook, over the flowers. Lollie walked slowly off the stage.

"To appear like that before Gustave," said Miss Ilse. "Your clothes all pulled round, not even as much as to pass a comb through your hair. How could you, Anna? I was so ashamed. You looked like a scarecrow, and before Gustave of all people."

"He didn't look at me," said Madame comfortably. "Ilse.

I have a feeling he will take them both. He will see Lion thoroughly tonight."

"Lion doesn't deserve it," said Miss Ilse, and pinched in her lips.

"He came back," said Madame.

"Yes, like a lord," said Miss Ilse. "Caroline . . ."

"Caroline." As she said it the happiness and excitement passed out of Madame's face.

"Hilda should move into Caroline's dressing-room," said Miss Ilse.

"She told you to ask for that?" said Madame quickly and suspiciously.

"No, she didn't, Anna."

"Tchk-tchk!" said Madame.

Miss Ilse led the way backstage and into the dressing-rooms. They paused in the narrow passage between the cubicles. As they paused, Lion came out. He was matt white, his eyes darkened and deepened by the kohl, his hair stiff with whitening. It was not dry and he had a towel on his shoulders. He stopped when he saw Madame.

"What are you doing here?" said Madame.

"I am just going on to let Noel see me again under the lights."

"I thought you had left my theatre, not?"

"No."

"No?"

"No."

"You are very firm."

"I am very firm," said Lion. He looked at her with warm deep affection in his eyes. "I carried you upstairs," he said. "Why are you standing about? Why do you let her stand?" he asked Miss Ilse, who gave an indignant little snort and went past them into Caroline's dressing-room.

"Caroline?" asked Madame.

Lion's eyes looked grave. Grave, not clouded as they did before when there was trouble, thought Madame. Grave and sorry.

"It's a pity about Caroline," said Lion. "I tried, but she wouldn't listen. I think she will be sorry," but the old Lion was not gone yet. "Do you know," he said confidentially, "I think Hilda is going farther than Caroline."

Madame went into Caroline's dressing-room. Caroline had taken her things away, but on the dressing-table was a litter of powder dust and face tissues and cotton-wool. There was wool on the floor, too, from her shoes. Miss Porteus was there, unpacking a box that was filled with tissue paper and from which a smell of camphor came. "What is that?" asked Madame.

"It's your dress of the Lady. Caroline's is too big for Hilda. It will need too much alteration. She will have to wear yours," said Miss Ilse.

"You should have asked me first," cried Madame.

They looked at her in astonishment. "Isn't it enough," cried Madame, "that she should oust . . . ?" They thought she meant Caroline, but she did not mean Caroline, or not only Caroline. Caroline was a small part of it. "Hilda is *not* to have my dress," said Madame. "Even if you sew oll night." She went to the box and touched the folded silk, an edge of embroidery, an ermine sleeve. "She is *not* to have my dress," she said. "Put it away."

"Take it upstairs, Miss Porteus," said Miss Ilse and, when Miss Porteus had gone, "You are wicked and ungrateful," she said to Madame. "When you think what Hilda has done."

"She should be grateful to me," flashed Madame. "Gustave . . ."

"Gustave! What would you have shown to Gustave but for Hilda?"

"It works both ways," argued Madame.

"It does indeed. Do you know what Hilda deserves?" asked Miss Ilse.

"She deserves anything I can give her," said Madame with sudden meekness.

"Then you should give her the Tsar's cross that Marli gave to you. *She* should have it, not Caroline."

"Yes," said Madame.

"And I shall fetch Zanny to get this room ready for Hilda," said Miss Ilse, dusting powder off the dressing-table.

"Yes," said Madame.

"Caroline will be sorry when she hears Gustave has been here," said Lion. He did not say it spitefully, but thoughtfully, as a fact to be regretted.

"Caroline deserves all she gets," said Miss Ilse, picking wool up from the floor.

"Yes," said Madame.

"Now I shall get Mrs. Pilgrim to sweep in here, and Zanny can move Hilda's things."

"Wait," said Madame suddenly. Miss Ilse looked up. Madame was standing in the doorway, her hand on Lion's arm. "Hilda doesn't need this dressing-room, Ilse," Madame pleaded. "Don't change anything, Ilse. Wait a little while. Lion, let Noel see you and then take oll this stuff off you and go to Caroline. Tell her what has happened, about Gustave, you understand. Then tell her . . . she is wanted by Madame."

Lion left Caroline with Madame and came back into the theatre. He met Hilda in the passage outside his dressing-room. She was dressed in the petticoats of the Second Pupil, with her sequined scarf wound round her. She was not made up, nor was her hair done, but tied back plainly with a white ribbon. She looked as plain as she had looked well that morning, but Lion did not know if she were plain or not. She was Hilda.

"Where have you been?" asked Lion.

"Having a bath," said Hilda. "I needed it."

Lion hesitated. "You . . . know . . . Caroline has come back?" He watched her to see how she would take it, but it did him no good. Hilda dropped her lids and he could gather nothing of how she felt. Hilda's reservations were up.

"Are you surprised?" he asked.

"Nothing that happens today will surprise me."

"Oh, well! You have plenty," said Lion. "Where are you off to? It's early. Where are you going?"

"Into the theatre."

"Can I come?"

"No."

"Hilda." He put his arm round her and felt her quiver under his touch, the reservations tottered.

"Lion. Please. Let me go."

"Why?"

"Because now, I . . . I want to be alone."

"Why?"

"Please, Lion."

"Kiss me, then."

"Not in the passage."

"In the passage."

She kissed him and suddenly she felt his lips quiver under the kiss; his, not hers. He . . . he cares, thought Hilda.

A new exultant certainty came into her.

"I . . . want to come with you," said Lion. She shook her head.

"I want to come," he said like a child.

"You can't," she said like a grownup, and gave him a gentle push away. She let her hand cling to his a moment and left him.

The florists had gone and the theatre bloomed with

flowers, banked along the stage, by the orchestra, and in the niches. Other flowers had been arriving all day and had been handed in to Emile and at the stage door. Except some for Caroline, few were for the company; they were for Madame: bunches and bouquets and baskets, a basket of red roses, a wreath of laurel leaves tied with a white ribbon. Telegrams were opened and pinned up on a notice-board; the telephone rang in the house and the box-office. Emile, Glancy, Mrs. Pilgrim, and the stage-hands came in and out of the theatre placing extra small gilt chairs that Miss Parkes had hastily sent for.

Miss Parkes, Rebecca, anyone that could be spared, were in the office amending the anniversary programmes with their crimson tassels. "First take out *Lyre*, put in those *Meditations*," said Rebecca. "Take out the *Meditations*. Put in *Leda and the Swan*. Then take out Caroline. Take out Lion. Put in Hilda. Put in Francis and Lippi. Take out Francis and Lippi. Put in Lion. Take out Hilda. Put in Caroline. I wish I had left at Christmas," said Rebecca.

Now, for a little while, the theatre was empty. Swept, filled with the scent of the flowers, it waited.

The curtain was down. Behind it the stage was set for *Cat Among the Pigeons*. In the dressing-rooms the freshly ironed clothes hung ready on the racks. The irons, still hot, were put to cool on the stands and Miss Porteus and Zanny toiled up and down carrying the dresses to the dressing-room. Wigs and jewellery and hats and caps hung on the mirrors; shoes were put ready in the shoe-holes under each stool. The dancers had brought in their good-luck charms and mascots, some serious, some ridiculous, and some sentimental. Madame's own were sentimental; she had always liked to have one red and one white rose in the vase on her table, and a certain little toy fan of white net with gold sequins that she had had as a child. She would never say who had given it to her. Perhaps she could not, now. The sequins were nearly worn away, but it and the roses were on her table tonight. "Ilse, you remembered them?"

"Of course I remembered them, Anna. We mustn't quarrel tonight."

"Quarrel! We *never* quarrel!" said Madame.

The girls had dolls or golliwoggs; some had teddy-bears; Alma had a Polish marionette and Rayevskaya a little Christmas tree with red wax buds. Gaby had an elephant's-hair bangle, Jessica a gold cross; "But you ought not to use that as a charm," Rayevskaya rebuked her. Francis had a sandalwood carving of Ganesh the Hindu god of success; when he heard Lion had come back, he turned Ganesh round with his face to the wall, but before he went on that evening he would run back and turn him round again . . . just in case. The branches of Rayevskaya's tree came across from her place at the mirror into Hilda's. Hilda had nothing at all. She felt her luck was in the theatre itself.

"How do you feel?" they had all asked her.

"I feel just the same."

"After Gustave . . . and your ballet. A ballet of your own with Gustave!"

She felt the same. She had always had these things in her. She had known that. It was only they who had not known. A week ago, yesterday, she might have said it. It was an older, wiser Hilda who held her tongue.

"But all in one day!" they said.

Not in one day. Years. Seventeen years. Ever since I was born, thought Hilda.

In the orchestra pit the lid was open on the piano, the clavichord for *The Noble Life* behind it; the harp stood to one side uncovered, its gilt strings shining in the one light Emile had left burning. He would come and turn the full lights on presently. It shone on the side of the cello and the bassoon, on the leather violin cases, on a silk handkerchief on one of the violinists' stands. The woodwind places were there, the music ready stacked, Mr. Felix's baton was on his stand. Will he bring his history book tonight? wondered Hilda. Or will he be a tiny bit interested? But then he says it is all history, she thought. Is it history? thought Hilda.

The light made a quiet pool on the cream walls, caught the angle of the blue stage curtains, the gilt rail, the cream and red and blue patternings of the orchestra curtains, a line of plush-backed seats, a gilt chair. It showed the colours of the gilt, the red plush and the flowers, the red and white carnations and the white jessamine. For the rest the theatre was dim, except out in the little foyer, where the chandelier was lit, shining in all its crystal ropes and pendants, reflected in the glass of the photographs on the walls and on the stand. Miss Ilse had changed the one of Giselle for

Giselle with marguerites. Hilda's sister had hurriedly brought down more photographs of Hilda. Caroline's and Lion's had been taken down, put up again. Now the foyer was quiet and in order, gleaming with light and filled with flowers. Emile had put the basket of roses under Madame's photograph on the stand; it was from Gustave. Later Gustave would lead her out before the audience on the stage, but now, for a few minutes, the theatre was alone, except for Hilda.

Outside in the road, the late afternoon light was growing richer as it drew towards evening. The rain had stopped and the ground steamed gently and Emile had put away the big canvas umbrella he had taken out. The smell of wet stone and earth and soot and brick and asphalt rose into the air, but the little theatre smelled inside and out of flowers. The sun lay on its façade, on the scrolled-iron balcony, the pendants of wistaria, and the new bills, still wet with printers' ink and limp with paste as Emile had put them up:

BALLETS HOLBEIN

Tonight at 7:00 and for a limited season

| *Cat Among the Pigeons* | *The Noble Life* |
| (Holbein) | (Holbein-Bellini) |

Leda and the Swan
(Hilda French)

Evenings at 7:00 Wed. Sat. 2:30

Holbein Theatre, Primrose Avenue, N.W. 3

To evoke is to call out, to draw out, and bring forth . . .

the dust of other seasons, other summers, other winters that, now they were evoked by this, shed their dust and came to life; other summers in other Mays, but with the same wistaria; winter seasons when Madame felt the wistaria should have been out, and another girl brought in just such a Christmas tree with red wax buds as Rayevskaya brought in now; other Rayevskayas, other Johns and Almas and Archies; other successful disappointed Lollies; other tears and other aspirations; other hates and other loves; other Hildas and other Lions.

Now a small queue began to form outside the gallery door, not yet opened. The dancers were slipping in, in ones and twos and threes, to make themselves up before they came down to warm up with Rebecca as was Madame's rule.

Caroline had come. She came from Madame and went to her dressing-room without a word to anyone, her head high. She too met Lion. Lion stepped back to let her pass and did not speak to her and she went into her dressing-room and shut the door.

On her table was a small package. It was from Madame. She recognized the careless sprawling writing. Caroline was still smarting from the things Madame had said, and she picked it up and put it down. Then she picked it up again and sprung open the lid warily, and diamonds sparkled up at her from rubies and she opened her lips in surprise. She read the note pinned to the velvet: *You have heard me speak of this often. It was given to me . . .*

Marli . . . the Tsar. . . . I had meant to keep it always . . . now you have come back to me . . . I want you to have it, Caroline. . . .

Lion met Caroline again. She had come out of her dressing-room in tights and practice dress. He thought she had been crying and he felt peacefully sorry for her. He had a peaceful utter friendliness for Caroline. It was peaceful not to want anything from her, not a place in Gustave's ballet, not even love. Of course I have all these things, he admitted, but it was true that Hilda had immunized him from his old practices. Now he paused. "Hullo," he said.

"Hullo," said Caroline.

"Where are you going?"

"To warm up with Rebecca."

"But . . ." Caroline's face warned him to stop. "But you are not on for nearly two hours."

"All the same," said Caroline, and she argued, "I can rest and warm up again."

Lion did not whistle nor show his surprise. He held out his hand. "I'm going to her too," he said. "Come along."

"Now you see, *if* I had put off Lollie's audition as you wanted me to, Ilse, as you tried to make me, this would never have happened. If I had not sat up oll night . . ."

"If Hilda had not written the ballet," said Miss Ilse dryly.

Candles were lit on Madame's dressing-table above her roses and her fan. "You make yourself up by candlelight and then it is all wrong," said Miss Ilse.

"Never mind. I like what I have to see best by candle-light, now I am old," said Madame.

She touched the roses. "I am old. There is no one to give these to me now, excepting you, Ilse."

"What nonsense," said Miss Ilse. "The whole theatre is overflowing with flowers."

Zanny was busy and Madame had been calling for Miss Ilse to hook her dress. "Where are you, Ilse? You are never, never here when I want you."

Miss Ilse had been going once more all through the theatre to see that it was all well, all arranged. Miss Ilse was not a participant, she was a part; a very necessary part. She had found a chair with a broken leg—"And imagine if anyone had sat on it!" She had had to mediate in a fight between Zanny and Archie's mother; and she had paused to watch the dancers working quietly with Rebecca.

"Can you imagine? Caroline was there!" she told Madame. "Caroline! Working with Rebecca!"

"Ah!" said Madame softly.

"And she was crying."

"Ah!" said Madame more softly still. "We shall have a very good performance from everyone tonight," she said. "I feel it. Sometimes, Ilse, I think, do you know what I think? I think I don't deserve so much goodness, so much happiness. I haven't forgotten how to manage, have I, Ilse? I couldn't manage the printers, but that was to be expected in these days. It is like the hole left to keep out the Evil Eye. There is some life left in me, not? *She always has something up her sleeve*. That was what Gustave said, not? And it is true. But I confess it to you, Ilse, I don't know myself what it was that I did for tonight. I don't know how it happened. It was a miracle, Ilse."

"I lit a candle to St. Jude," said Miss Ilse, to explain the miracle.

"Don't talk such nonsense, Ilse. You are a fool. St. Jude! It might have been Lollie and the audition and Edmund bringing Gustave . . . but if we had not done *Leda and the Swan,* what would he have seen? If I had not sat up oll night and found it, we should not have had *Leda and the Swan.* If Felix had not helped . . . if Noel had not come . . . and we mustn't forget Edwin and Zanny and Miss Porteus and, even, Glancy. They have oll worked well, oll of them; we must not grudge it them. If they call me on the stage tonight, and they *may* call me, Ilse, not? . . ."

"Of course they will call you, Anna."

"Then I shall call them oll. Oll. Every one of them. From Caroline and Lion, down to them oll."

"I think you should call Hilda, first, by herself."

Madame was silent. She said slowly, "I shall have to call Hilda. I shall call her and then . . . I shall leave the stage. To her. By herself. Yes. I shall have to do that. It is rright." It was right, but it was still disagreeable. "Hilda will not stay with us," she said. "There is nothing more for her here. Yes. We have served her purpose," said Madame. It was bitter, but it was a fact. She had thought of Caroline as a meadow and that was right; now she could see the bounds of Caroline, but she could not tell how far Hilda would go; she knew that Hilda had passed her and was going out of sight. "Tonight, for me, is perhaps the end," she said, "but for Hilda it is only a milestone." She had again, and not even finally, that same jealous rebel pang. "Tchk-tchk!" said Madame. "Ilse, will you hook my dress, not? What are you standing there for? It is late and everybody will be waiting. What are you thinking of?" She paused and said, "Still, I don't know what it was. Not one thing by itself, but the way it all turned out, not? I wonder what it was," said Madame.

And Miss Ilse said, as she bent to hook the dress, "It was my candle to St. Jude."